# Confessions of a Greedy Girl

## MADELYNNE ELLIS

*Mischief*
An imprint of HarperCollins*Publishers*
77–85 Fulham Palace Road,
Hammersmith, London W6 8JB

www.mischiefbooks.com

A Paperback Original 2013

First published in Great Britain in ebook format by
HarperCollins*Publishers* 2012

A catalogue record for this book is
available from the British Library

ISBN-13: 9780007553389

Find out more about HarperCollins and the environment at
**www.harpercollins.co.uk/green**

# CONTENTS

| | |
|---|---|
| Chapter One | 1 |
| Chapter Two | 29 |
| Chapter Three | 43 |
| Chapter Four | 59 |
| Chapter Five | 72 |
| Chapter Six | 91 |
| Chapter Seven | 104 |
| Chapter Eight | 127 |
| Chapter Nine | 143 |
| Chapter Ten | 152 |
| Chapter Eleven | 177 |

# Chapter One

'Lyssa! You could at least pretend to be listening while I'm telling you about my abysmal date. The odd acknowledgement wouldn't hurt. Even a grunt, so I'm actually convinced you're still alive.'

'Huh? What?' I glanced up from the theatre seating plan I'd been colouring for the last half-hour – red for empty seats, blue for those that had already been reserved, and green for the corporate bookings – to find my favourite workmate glowering at me. The only trouble with working in the theatre box office was that it was either all go, phones ringing, people hammering on the window for attention, or else afternoons of endless, coma-inducing nothingness. Programmes didn't need stapling, ice-cream didn't need ordering, and even the drinks tickets for tonight's interval were already printed. Of course I'd zoned out. 'Sorry, Hats. I didn't mean to ignore you. Go on, you were saying you touched him, right?'

Hattie scrunched two handfuls of her naturally jet-black

1

hair and sighed. 'Jeez, Lyssa, you really weren't listening, were you? Point one: the main focus of a first date is not to cop a feel of a guy's tackle. Point two: Bryan never even kissed me. There's no way he'd have let me grope him. We didn't even shake hands.'

Surprised, and not entirely on board with Hattie's version of dating, I plastered on a sheepish grin that would hopefully diffuse some of Hattie's anger. When roused she bore a certain similarity to a Chinese firecracker, and she could be vicious with a staple gun.

'It turns out he has obsessive compulsive disorder. It means he has to disinfect after he comes into contact with anything foreign. We lasted twenty minutes before I called it off. I couldn't take the scent of alcohol gel any longer.'

'OK. I can see how that might have caused some problems.' It'd definitely rule out anything similar to the night I'd enjoyed at the gallery. Though I'd suffered for it the following morning, and it'd left me wondering about several things. How could a man be so into me, but not want to touch me? I didn't suppose I'd ever find out. It wasn't as if we'd exchanged numbers, and even if we had, I wouldn't have expected him to call.

'But you did say you were kissing someone, right? I swear I distinctly heard the K word mentioned.'

Hattie's pretty almond-shaped eyes narrowed to two thin slits. 'No, all I did was speculate what it might be like to actually date someone I fancied for a change, rather than the losers DatesRUs keep pairing me with.'

'Oh, Hats.' I hid my smile. She really didn't need a match making service, and certainly not one with such a dire name. Hattie was lovely; delicate and refined in the way only the Chinese seemed to manage. All she needed to do was lower her standards from the heights of perfection they were currently set upon, or failing that get a guy home with her long enough to experience her cooking. I'd tasted her dumplings – and sworn undying love to her shortly afterwards.

'Seriously, Lyssa why does it have to be so hard? You never have any trouble finding yourself a nice guy. I know you have Nathan now, but even before him there was always a steady stream. You never wanted for a date if you fancied a night out.'

'Hm.' Only partly true. My list of exes included the jobless, the homeless, an entrepreneur and an investment banker. None of whom had been great choices. I certainly had bad memories about coming second in importance to a sock empire. 'I'm not exactly choosy,' I reminded her.

'So you're saying I have to lower my standards.' Hattie pursed her cute little Cupid's bow lips and thought for a moment, before dismissing the advice. 'I don't think I can do it. I mean, he needs to be fit and at least reasonably good looking for starters. And he can't smell. Plus, he has to be able to hold a conversation about more than

Smartphone apps and sport. But I don't want a geeky professor either.'

She really didn't ask for much.

'And good in the bedroom department,' I suggested.

'And good in the –' Hattie's lips twisted into a puckered moue. 'I'm not bothered about that. As long as he knows where to put it, we'll be fine.'

'Right.' I nodded tactfully, what was point in discussing this when I knew she already had her heart set on the impossible? Sure enough, Hattie's gaze strayed to the huge black and white close-up of Leif Haralsson that sat directly opposite the booking desk. There was no denying the theatre's current male lead oozed style. Every inch of his tall, wiry frame was perfection. He looked fab in clothes. He probably looked even better out of them. Couple that with his soft, candid blue eyes, a bird's nest of light blond hair, and he was a female fantasy made flesh.

Nor did his sexiness end there. Nope, he had a voice that flowed through one's veins as if you'd just injected chocolate, a sharp-edged jaw with a cute little cleft in his chin, and the sort of sultry pout hitherto only seen on old-time screen legends. Did I want to screw him? Absolutely. Did Hattie stand a chance? Probably not, if only because she'd have to wade through a ton of adoring fans with far looser morals to get to him.

'You know he doesn't have a girlfriend,' Hattie

confided, her voice becoming soft and just a little breathless. 'Melanie from wardrobe told me.'

Melanie, the fount of all wisdom, had probably forgotten to mention that he was a) gay, b) married or c) both. Still, so as not to dishearten my one true friend, I patted her on the back. 'Fab. So ask him out.'

'Really?' Hattie snapped to attention. 'I suppose I could, couldn't I?' Sometimes she forgot this was the twenty-first century. 'That's how you hooked up with Nathan, wasn't it? You asked him out.'

'Pretty much.' I ducked my head. The problem with discussing men was that the conversation inevitably seemed to come round to my love life. If love life had been an accurate descriptive, that wouldn't have mattered, but what I had was actually a sex life, and a fairly unusual one at that. I was swinging with three guys and a couple, four if you counted the man I'd met at the gallery, and Hattie only knew about Nathan. As for how I'd hooked up with Nathan, the problem there started with the word 'date'. Date hadn't featured very prominently in our first conversation, and certainly hadn't preceded 'fuck', 'ride', or 'cock', and possibly hadn't come before 'you don't mind if my mate joins in, do you?' either.

I could be a really bad girl.

I was also a monumental coward. 'Hey, I'm going to go and straighten up the gift section.' It had already been done that morning, but anything to avoid the relationship questions. I liked Hattie – a lot. I didn't want to fall out with her, but I'd learned pretty quickly that people didn't like my arrangement. While one or two friends had been accepting, more often they turned judgemental, and then cut me dead. The friends I had remaining were mostly the ones I was playing with, and even they were slightly huffy with me at the moment. It wasn't as if I'd planned what had happened at the gallery, I'd just been swept along by events. Birthday madness, I suppose you could call it ...

Let me explain first that pottery doesn't excite me. The choice of venue for my birthday outing wasn't of my choosing, but the tickets had been free and so was the booze, so I could hardly complain. Nor did the mono-chrome palette of this particular pottery collection help to inspire any new-found love. So it's surely not much of a surprise to learn that when Nathan quirked his eyebrow and in his best James Bond voice asked if I'd prefer to be shaken or stirred I accepted his offer to find out.

We were giggling when we crept into the gallery's green room, having completely ignored the sign that read 'VIPs only'. It was already late in the evening at this point, and I'd drunk far too much champagne. I was feeling pleasantly tipsy. My inhibitions had sailed west and, I'll admit, I was spectacularly failing to keep my hands off Nathan's glorious butt. You see he'd scrubbed up rather well tonight. Out had gone his normal weathered jeans, replaced by smart black trousers, and a tuxedo and bow tie. I never could resist a smartly dressed man, and booze makes me horny.

I expected the green room to be just as dull and austere as the rest of the gallery, with its whitewashed concrete and steel design, but much to my delight, that wasn't the case. Instead, we stepped into a world of glittering black tiles, huge gilt-framed mirrors and mood lighting. Someone with comfort in mind had designed this room. Several sumptuous red leather sofas completed the effect. But, best of all, the room was deserted.

'Finally.' Nathan ushered me inside and closed the door. His arms immediately wrapped around my waist from behind. 'Which was it you said you preferred – shaken, or stirred?' He jogged me about a bit, making me squeal, but bringing us into closer contact. Breathless with laughter, I snuggled against his warmth. 'What say I give you a little birthday treat?'

I didn't have to look at him to know what he had in mind. It was on my mind too.

'We shouldn't,' I gushed, while relishing the prospect of being naughty. 'Someone might come in.'

'Really, no? Or do you just mean, tempt me some more?' He fitted himself to the curve of my back and began to roll our hips together in a slow dance. 'Who's going to catch us? Folk were already leaving when we sneaked off. There's probably only Sam and David left in the building by now.' Sam was the gallery's assistant manager, David her husband, one of the directors. In fact, Sam had provided the tickets for the exhibition. 'You know neither of them would object to us having a little fun.' His whisky-gold eyes glinted with wicked intent as he held my gaze via the mirror.

True enough, they were more likely to join in than protest. Still, this was a public building, even if it were a private lounge within it, and everyone else had gone home.

'What about if I just creep under here a little?' Nathan walked his fingers up my thigh, so that his hand found its way under the short hem of my dress. I clamped a hand down to stop his progress, but Nathan was one step ahead. His lips teased the shell of my ear in the exact way that's guaranteed to undo me. Right on cue, a pleasant shiver rolled through my body, leaving me tingly and alert, and I forgot all about playing hard to get. 'Let's live a little, Lys. You only get to be twenty-seven once, remember.'

True enough. I kept promising myself I wasn't going to grow old and boring. I'd already wasted too many years being young and boring. Ever since I'd split with my ex, three days into the New Year, I'd been making up for lost time. A moment later, Nathan's fingers alighted someplace they oughtn't to have been, prompting another sharp intake of breath.

'Here or outside,' he hissed. 'There's no way I can wait until I get you home. Got to have you soon, babe.' His lips found mine, and I could only agree. Thoughts of cleaners and security staff were pushed to the very back of my brain. No one would walk in, and even if they did, so what. He was sexy and I was more than eager to feel what he'd got.

Nathan didn't waste any time. He rocked forward a fraction, sliding our bodies into closer contact, while our tongues continued to duel.

'Mm.' I wriggled back against his hard-on, while our tongues continued to duel, and gasped to find his fly already loose.

Nathan chuckled against my shoulder. 'God, you're sexy when you do that. Do it again?'

I wasn't sure if he meant the groan or the wiggle, so I did both. 'Someone's eager.'

'Babe, I'm so hard, I'm aching.' He nudged my knees apart, and slipped himself between my thighs. Hard muscle stroked along the seam of my pussy. Heat immediately filled my cheeks.

Whoa! I hadn't realised my desire had become quite so acute. I was wet and slick, and more than a little warm. 'Yes,' I encouraged, trying to angle my hips in order to capture him more fully. 'More.'

'Babe, you're so soft and warm.' He trembled a little, as he tried to hold me steady. It didn't work, I was just too eager, and feeling him there, right between my thighs, mere millimetres from where I wanted to get him, was proving too much. 'Yeah,' he sighed, sliding against me. 'Just, yeah.'

When the door swung open, I had sense enough left to try and push Nathan off. He, of course, was having none of it. Thankfully, the intruder turned out to be David, with Sam not far behind.

'I told you we'd find them somewhere they weren't supposed to be, being inappropriate,' David remarked.

'And I agreed, if you recall. Honestly, you two. Can't you keep your hands off one another for a second?' Sam cast a stern glance in our direction before giving her husband a hungry kiss, hands already groping his body.

'If we did, she'd be horribly disappointed,' Nathan whispered into my ear. He was right. Despite having their hands inside one another's clothing, they'd stopped kissing in order to watch us. I didn't understand David and Sam, but that didn't stop me enjoying their company. Despite being married, or maybe because of it, they seemed to prefer participating in other people's pleasure rather than seeking their own with one another. Nathan had introduced them to me shortly after we'd first met. They were his favourite neighbours, a few years his senior, but always ready to indulge his particular quirk. They loved watching and Nathan loved being watched.

'You planned this,' I realised. A grin stretched wide

across my lips, as I turned my gaze between Sam and then Nathan. That's how Nathan had known how to find this place. Sam had given him directions.

She lifted her shoulders in admission. 'Well, we couldn't let your birthday pass without a little celebration, and we figured you hadn't come up here before.' Her smile told me the double entendre had been deliberate. 'You don't mind us being here, do you, Lyssa?'

'No.' What else was I supposed to say?

'Good.' Sam stepped out of her underwear, before settling on one of the sofas. Nathan, meanwhile, nudged me forwards towards another. Thanks to the mirrors, we could all still see one another from numerous angles. I could see why Sam and David liked this room, and I suspected this wasn't the first performance they'd watched up here.

On the plus side, their presence had kicked any residual fear of discovery I had left. If we'd been in any danger, Sam wouldn't have taken her knickers off!

'Lift her dress, Nathan,' she instructed. 'Let us see if you've worked any magic yet.'

He flicked my dress up high, so it was gathered around my waist, giving everyone a good look at my stocking tops and the teeny scrap of fabric that passed for my underwear. The triangle of which was already embarrassingly wet.

'Looks as if she's pretty eager.'

11

'Fairly.' Still behind me, Nathan wetted his lips. 'I think there's just one little thing I need to do.' He bent, but not to dress for action, as I supposed. Instead, his lips pressed to one cheek of my bottom, shocking and electrifying me. Nathan knew how sensitive my bottom was. Kisses there could drive me near insane. He wasn't content with only bestowing kisses either. His devil's tongue dabbed wickedly between the cheeks, seeking out the furl of muscle hidden there.

'Nathan! Oh ...' I was pretty sure women could die from what he could do with his tongue. Considering the speed of my pulse, I was about to become the first casualty.

'Is he? Oh, my God, he is,' David blurted, before Sam hushed him. One glance from the corner of my eye confirmed what my ears had already told me. They were enjoying the display on a mental as well as physical level.

'Nathan, no,' I crooned. Some things were meant to be done in privacy, and this was surely one of them. It wasn't that I was inexperienced, or embarrassed, only that I couldn't control my reaction if he was teasing me like this. I knew I'd end up thrashing about, and screaming God knows what for everyone to hear. They didn't need to hear me yelling, 'Harder. Deeper.'

'Spoilsport.' Nathan relinquished, and kissed his way up my back, returning his attention to my earlobe again. 'Suppose I'll have to content myself with this

12

little peach instead.' His hand covered my pussy and squeezed. 'Ready?' It wasn't really a question. He was already pushing in.

'There now. There,' he muttered, at my gasp.

Boy, did it feel good. Tight and glorious. The slow, easy roll of his hips alongside mine was coupled with the brush of his fingers against my breasts. 'So, so, good.' So good, in fact, that it took a minute or two to realise he was holding back. Typically, Nathan went at it hard, exactly the way I liked him too. His current thrusts weren't nearly deep, or swift enough to truly please.

'Don't sulk,' I hissed.

'I'm not. I just wanted a piece of your arse.'

'Later,' I promised. Once we were home and safely behind locked doors. Apparently, the promise was incentive enough. He immediately picked up the pace.

'Harder?' His fingers tightened around my shoulder providing leverage. 'More like this, huh?'

God, yes! Exactly like that. Adrenaline rushed through me like I'd been dropped from a hundred feet and swung through a few loop-the-loops. The sofa hammered against the wall as our bodies smacked together, so that in seconds we were both breathless and lathered.

'Not – sure – how – much – of – this – I – can – take.' Nathan's words punched free of his throat in time with his thrusts. It was going to be quick. Very quick. Nathan could go like a jackhammer, but he was a sprinter, not a marathon runner. He often burned himself out before I'd properly warmed through. Luckily, he had no issues about sharing me. He was quite happy for another guy to finish me off, if he was spent. Still, my other lovers weren't here tonight, and this was fast, even for Nathan.

'Don't you dare,' I warned him when arrhythmia started to creep in to his motion.

'Dare what?' His fingers curved possessively against my bottom. 'I reckon I know who's going to come first tonight, and it definitely ain't me.' He mischievously brushed his thumb along the channel between my cheeks, making the furled muscle he'd previously kissed twitch with excitement. 'Knock, knock, let me in.' One digit, then a second slipped past the gate, sending a shockwave of pleasure up my spine. In seconds my legs were jelly. But, in the end, it wasn't that, but Nathan's thumb stroking across my painfully hard clit that set me off.

One touch and I was gone; body convulsing, and sucking up Nathan's orgasm like it was oxygen and I was starved of air.

Shaken and giddy – I hadn't thought Nathan meant to be so literal – I sagged against the sofa back, content to let the aftershocks ripple through me. Nathan, however, had other plans. He pulled out, only to push into my rear.

'God, Nathan.' My sex was still rippling with pleasure. I didn't have the will to shove him away. But, even though he entered me gradually, it was still torment and bliss rolled into one. The sensations were exquisitely raw. The tightness, the way he rubbed against all of my most tender nerve endings, enough to make my hair curl.

That didn't mean I wasn't going to give him a right earful once he was done. 'God, I love you, you're such a dirty pair,' I heard either Sam or David mumble. I tried not to look at them to work out which, knowing if I did my cheeks would heat with shame, and that alone might tip me over. A second climax was already boiling up inside of me.

The shadow seemed like nothing at first – just a flaw in the mirror, or a trick of the lighting.

Even when he stared at me, I didn't think that he was real, just an illusion – a sultry ghost with thick dark hair and chin carved from granite, dressed in a vintage velvet jacket and cravat, like he'd been plucked right out of 1964. A real person would have made a fuss. Yet, he acted as if it were routine to see a girl taken thus.

Warning bells jangled as he strolled over to the coffee machine.

When actual water spluttered from the nozzle, my heart nearly stopped.

As a group, we made a collective yelp. Nathan froze mid-stroke.

'Aw, hell!' Sam jolted out of her chair. 'Oh, my God, Victor! Mr Alexander. I'm so sorry. I had no idea you were still here.' Sam hastily rearranged her bunched up skirt. The cerise taffeta refused to fall in to place, leaving all of her coltish legs on display.

'No, no. Don't apologise. Carry on.' The man, whose name had been on every banner in the gallery, gave a dismissive wave before reaching for his brew.

'No, really …' Sam continued to apologise. 'Um … I think we ought to be going. Come along now, everybody out. Let Mr Alexander have his peace.'

'There's really no need.' A twitch of annoyance flashed across his face. It seemed Victor Alexander was more perturbed by Sam's insistence that we stop, than by the depravity he'd stumbled upon. Having finished making his drink, he turned and rested against the arm of the sofa Sam had jumped up from, and from which David was still extracting himself.

'What are you doing?' Sam asked, the quaver in her voice betraying her still underlying panic.

Victor raised his eyebrows. 'Watching. Drinking my coffee. Given how much you were enjoying yourselves it must be a good show.'

Is it wrong that I loved him from that very moment, from his winkle-pickers to his mod jacket to his almost, but not quite perfect nose? I slapped a hand across my mouth to hide my smile, while Sam gaped and spluttered. I probably ought to have tried to extract myself from the situation, rather than stand there being amused, with my butt on show, but Nathan held me in a death grip.

'No – no. You can't.' Sam reached out to her celebrity guest, but stopped short of dragging him from his perch. 'I thought you'd left. I watched you go.' She finally managed to wrench her dress into the correct position, at which point her cool, business self reasserted itself. She took a breath, and spoke calmly, 'I'll go and order you a taxi now. I apologise things weren't properly organised earlier.' She took a step towards the door, then abruptly backtracked and grabbed hold of her husband. David was still fastening his fly as she dragged him into the corridor.

'We ought to leave too,' Nathan murmured into my ear. His grip had relaxed a fraction, allowing me the freedom to move. 'Ease forward slowly. We don't need to show him anything.'

Curiously, the thought of Victor's gaze upon my naked bottom sparked excitement rather than horror. I actually didn't mind that he wanted to watch. Interesting, considering Nathan, the man who usually loved being watched, was itching to get away.

'Lyssa,' Nathan prompted.

'I meant it. Don't feel you have to spoil your fun because of me,' Victor remarked. If the fun hadn't already been over, I might have taken him at his word, but Nathan's erection had shrunk and was now safely tucked up behind his fly.

'Another time,' I said, as if we were likely to cross paths again under similar circumstances.

'Definitely.' Victor flashed me a sinful smile, showing just a hint of teeth that seemed to convert my throwaway remark into a promise.

'What the devil did you say that for?' Nathan barked, once he'd bundled me into the corridor. 'Lord knows what sort of nutcase you've encouraged. Next thing you know he'll be stalking you.' I didn't think Victor was a nutcase, but Nathan barely let me get a word in until we'd reached the foyer, and then only to enquire if I had everything before we got into the waiting taxi. I was willing to bet it was meant for Victor, but Nathan didn't seem to care.

'Actually, no.' I paused at the top of the entrance steps, forcing Nathan to backtrack in order to find out what the problem was. As a consequence of being dragged from the room, I'd managed to leave my handbag behind. 'Purse,' I explained.

'Oh, blinking hell, Lys!'

'It's not your problem,' I snarled back.

'Get in the cab. I'll fetch it.'

I nearly did, until I realised going home sans keys and cash would be completely pointless. 'You get in,' I insisted. 'My keys are in my purse.' That and it plain made more sense for me to fetch my bag. I knew where I'd left it for starters, and nor was I quite so desperate to flee into the night. 'Go home, Nathan. I'll get Sam to phone me another taxi. We'll catch up later in the week.'

For a moment I thought he was going to be belligerent about it. Nathan could be remarkably stubborn on occasion. His eyebrows were drawn low and his lips had formed a sour line. 'Go. Honest, I'll be fine.' I was a big girl and I knew how to find my way home. Nor was I half as tipsy as I'd been an hour ago.

'Oi! You getting in, or what, mate?' the cabbie hollered.

'All right,' Nathan gave in with a sigh. He kissed my cheek. 'I'll see you Friday. Stay safe.' He clearly wasn't pleased to be leaving me behind, but he got into the cab.

I was already back inside the building by the time they pulled away.

Victor occupied almost exactly the same spot I'd stood in moments before when I returned to the green room. He turned slowly when he saw my reflection so that we were facing when I walked towards him. 'I forgot my purse,' I explained.

He bent and retrieved the item from the sofa, then held it out to me.

'Thanks.'

'No problem.'

Really, that's where the conversation ought to have ended. Except, let's just say that on second inspection, my interest was doubly piqued.

Victor Alexander was not a traditionally handsome man, but he was definitely a striking one. It was more than just his clothes. He was slender as a willow, and angular, almost to the point of being gangly, with thick collar-length black hair. Yet it was his very loose-limbed eccentricity that made him interesting. What captured me at that moment though, were his eyes – eyes full of icy flames. Looking at him made me believe in Jack Frost and the Snow Queen, and conjured images of ice palaces and romping before roaring fires wrapped in bearskins.

What's more, not only did I suddenly want to inhabit those snowy vistas with him; I suspected he felt exactly the same way.

'Was there something else?' he asked in response to my lack of movement.

'No, that's everything.' I shook myself out of my stupor and tucked my purse under one arm. 'Well, goodbye again,' I remarked, turning away.

'You know it really wasn't my intention to spoil your birthday.'

I turned back again, and he nodded towards the ridiculous pink birthday badge Nathan had insisted on pinning to my dress.

'That's OK. You haven't – yet.'

'Yet?' He grinned and I couldn't help but reciprocate. 'That rather implies that I'm about to.' He sat down, so I did too.

'Depends,' I remarked cryptically. God knows what I was thinking, but considering the way he was making my insides fizz just by looking at me, I'd be a fool not to try to draw this out.

He pressed his index finger across his lips. 'On what?'

'Whether you're going to kiss me?' Now I was being downright naughty, perhaps even too outrageous for his sensibilities. Really, I knew nothing about him. The thing was I'd seen this film once, where the girl says to the guy 'we should have sex', within minutes of meeting him. And they do. And then they keep meeting and it all turns out wonderfully. Based on first impressions, I think I was hoping for a similar kind of happily-ever-after with this man. That was assuming I hadn't already convinced him I was delusional, desperate and/or dangerous. Lord knows it was probably justified. I'd only just met the man, and I'd just sent my date home in a taxi. Not that Nathan and I were a proper item.

'I'm not sure I can do that, Lyssa.'

I heard the words, but it was his expression I paid attention to. He never once looked away. 'Even if I say please?' Daringly, I touched his face.

'Even if you say pretty please.' He didn't attempt to escape my touch, though he did put his hand over mine. I bit my lip. I guess I'd read the whole thing wrong and had somehow misconstrued his politeness for genuine interest, and yet … Dammit, I leaned forward to steal what I wanted. He tasted good. It felt even better.

He looked slightly shocked, but not in an angry way.

Taking that as encouragement, I leaned forward to do it again. Victor covered his mouth with his fingers. Instead of kissing, we stared at one another from a distance of mere inches.

'I can't.'

'Nathan and I, we're not committed,' I explained, thinking that might be the reason for his reluctance. He had just witnessed me being taken by the guy. 'What I mean is that we're lovers, but we're not in love. We're not exclusive. We see other people.' I'm not sure my explanation was really helping.

'I still can't.'

'Girlfriend?' I wondered aloud.

'No.'

'Married?' Not that he was wearing a ring, but not all guys do.

He shook his head.

Well, I guess I'd made a big enough fool of myself. I made to rise, only for him to catch hold of my hand. My insides were flip-flopping between precaution and desire, as he drew me back down onto the sofa, but I knew what was going to happen. I was going to have sex with this man. Sizzling hot, uncomplicated, birthday sex and it was going to be terrific.

'I'm curious, do you make a habit of flaunting yourself and then propositioning the onlookers?'

'Do you make a habit of spying on people?'

'Touché.'

Goddammit, what were we doing. He was still holding my hand, and smoothing circles over my knuckles with his thumb. How could I feel so turned on by something so simple?

'Nathan stole your cab, by the way.'

'Did he?' He didn't seem overly concerned by the fact. 'I guess that means I'm stuck here a little longer.'

Considering he'd just refused to kiss me, he made that remark sound awfully like a proposition.

'And?' I prompted. Something had to happen. I couldn't sit here feeling this tense without completely losing my mind.

'And –' His smile grew impossibly broad. '– and I'm sorry I missed the opportunity to see you –'

'– to see me?'

'Come,' he said.

Heat rushed through me like I'd been hit by a geyser. I was stunned by his words and simultaneously aflame. My body gave one pulse after another, while between my thighs I was suddenly sodden. I'd never had such a strong reaction to a single word before. I didn't actually come, but I came insanely close.

'Maybe you could touch yourself?'

OK, I thought I'd been forward for stealing kisses, but he was demanding far more.

'Where exactly?' As if the direction of his gaze didn't

make it obvious. 'You can't expect me to do that here?'

'Why's it any different to what you were doing earlier?'
When he put it like that, he sort of had a point. I'd still
be getting off in public with an audience. It's just that
doing myself seemed far naughtier than doing it with
another person, and I at least knew Sam and David,
whereas I knew nothing about him. Of course, that hadn't
stopped me trying to jump his bones a minute ago. Nor
was I particularly shy about this sort of thing. I wasn't
the kind of girl who never touched herself. I often used
my fingers to help things along. Plus, there was every
possibility that if I did this, he'd be all over me as hard
as I could possibly wish.

I sat back and, knees bent, opened my legs a fraction,
just enough so that he could see up my dress. Tentatively,
I put one hand on my thighs, and raised it along with
the hem of my dress.

Victor's gaze became fully focussed on the ascent of my
fingertips. He crept forward, first perching on the sofa
edge, then kneeling on the floor to watch as I brushed
through the tufts of dark curling hair framing my sex.
Considering how aroused I already was, I kept the touches
light, and well away from anything sensitive.

'I bet you're really good with your hands, being a
sculptor.'

The prompt failed to draw him. If he'd just move one
of his hands slightly so that it lay upon my thigh.

'Potter,' he corrected. 'Sculptors carve. They chip away at things. I mould things to my will.'

I could believe that, although, presently I was more interested in getting my hands on his body and exploring all of his curious male angles and ridges, than letting him top me. Instinct told me he possessed the sort of washboard abs you could climb down, and I had high hopes for other bits too, given the bulge he was sporting.

'Why don't you touch properly?' he asked, reasonably.

'Because I'm wound too tight.' I'd come too fast and too hard, when I wanted to draw this out. 'Surely you know how that feels.' An erection as fierce as the one he had caged had to hurt. 'Maybe you should ... as well.'

Our gazes met. Raw lust crackled between us. I read his need. How he longed to bury himself deep, pound into me until there were no boundaries left between us, and we burned with pure lust. I saw too that he wouldn't do it. Victor Alexander had no intention of doing me, even if that meant he had to ride home with a hard-on you could bang nails with. He wouldn't give in. Not tonight, and as far as I could read, not any time soon either.

For some mad reason, he'd decided not to touch me or himself.

'Do you usually just get off by watching?'

'Not as a rule.

'Touch yourself there,' he demanded.

My fingers were trembling, my agility shot to pieces. It

was like a battle of wills. Both of us staring. I'm not sure who gasped the loudest when I finally did as he asked. My little bud stood so far to attention that one press there was like hitting the ignition on an explosive device. And once done, there was no going back. I couldn't stop. I couldn't unwind the act.

Victor remained unearthly still. He didn't rub himself. He didn't even twist to generate friction. He just let his yearning fill up his expression, until it became too raw to look at, too mesmerising and terrifying. I didn't understand it, but I felt its lure.

My eyelids fluttered closed. The darkness only increased my awareness of him; his thick earthy scent, the whisper of his breath against my hot skin. He moved. Blew. My body convulsed. He blew again and orgasm gripped me tight. Without touching me, Victor tipped me over. I came so hard the muscles in my thighs were still twitching minutes afterwards.

I opened my eyes to find him still there, still watching me with those silver-grey eyes, while his breath continued to whisper across my sex, now soothing instead of teasing. 'Beautiful,' he muttered.

He offered me a hand up, which I accepted, thinking that now surely I'd be rewarded with a kiss.

Apparently not.

'Why?' I had to ask.

He had to know he could do whatever he wanted to

me at that moment. Instead, he stood away from me, tense and horny, when really there was no need. I could make him feel good.

'I've probably kept you too long.' He shoved his hands into his pockets, which had the effect of raising his shoulders.

'That's fine. You know I don't normally —'

'You don't have to explain.'

But I did. I didn't want him to think I routinely picked up guys in this way. Yes, I enjoyed a somewhat unconventional sex life, but I only really played with guys I knew. I'm not saying I hadn't enjoyed the odd one-night stand in the past, but it wasn't my normal mode of operation.

'We'd better go down now, in case there's another taxi waiting.'

A curious combination of embarrassment and relief flickered across Sam's face when she saw us together. I was betting she'd anticipated me having left along with Nathan. 'I was just coming to find you,' she said to Victor. 'The taxi just pulled up.' We headed straight outside.

'Are you OK sharing?' I asked.

'It's yours. My lift's finally arrived.' He glanced across the car park to a point some distance away. 'It was nice meeting you.'

'Likewise.'

He lingered, rather than hurrying away. 'Why aren't

you an item?' he asked, referring back to my remarks about Nathan.

'I'm not sure I could ever be content with only one man.' I was being flippant. The hour was late and I still didn't know how to interpret him. The truth was that I was still carrying around too much baggage from my last relationship to consider confining myself to another man anytime soon. Craig and I had split after he accused me of infidelity. All I'd actually done was ogle a few guys. Not touched them or kissed them, just turned my head to look when they walked by. In Craig's eyes that was enough.

At least my present arrangement allowed me to do whatever I wanted with whoever I chose. It kept things simple.

'What about you?' I asked, as he held open the taxi door so I could climb inside.

An enigmatic grin spread across his face. 'One man is plenty.'

# Chapter Two

We weren't really supposed to carry personal phones at work, but I'd accidentally left mine in my pocket earlier, so when it bleeped as I worked on tidying up the jewellery stand, I took it out and answered.

'Hello.'

'Lyssa?'

I knew his voice at once. 'Victor?' I clutched the phone so tight to my ear it began to ache. Oh, my God. Oh, my God. How had he got my number? Why had he called? 'I wasn't expecting to hear from you?'

'Your friend Sam gave me your number. She wasn't happy about it, so I had to twist her arm. I don't think she likes me anymore.'

'Oh!' A nervous giggle escaped my mouth. I could guess what sort of persuasion he'd used. 'But you wouldn't really have exposed her,' I said, as I ducked out of sight behind one of the display racks.

It was Victor's turn to laugh. 'As what – a woman

with a sex life? Come on, I'm equally, if not more, guilty of public lewdness than she is.'

'You didn't take any clothes off,' I reminded him. He hadn't done anything besides watch, much to my chagrin. I wanted to ask him why, but the moment didn't feel right. I was too curious to learn why he'd phoned to risk him hanging up.

'You know –' I could practically imagine him ticking one of his long elegant fingers at me '– I'm not sure that would weigh much in my defence, given the view from where I was standing.'

'My view was pretty good too.'

'Was it?'

Damn, now I was blushing. I held my breath, waiting to hear why he'd called.

'Can we meet?' he asked.

Yes! Yes, we most certainly could. 'When?' I gasped, so urgently I probably sounded like a slavering beast.

'How about tonight?'

Argh! It was Friday. I already had arrangements for tonight. I danced about from one foot to the other. To anyone walking past I probably looked like a toddler desperate for a pee. Ultimately though, there was only one answer I could give, despite how little I wanted to give it. 'I'm sorry, Victor. I can't. I'd love to. It's just I have something on.'

'You mean you're seeing someone else.'

It was a standing arrangement that I met the guys on a Friday night. We had fun. We got inventive. This evening's entertainment had been planned for weeks. 'We're playing laser tag. Nathan's picking me up.'

'Excuse me?' His disbelief whistled out of the speaker.

'It's where you chase around and try to zap one another.' We didn't only meet up for sex. OK, maybe we did, but at least we tried to be original about it.

'I know what it is, Lyssa. Humour me; I'm trying to picture you in combat boots and camos. Do you have one of those little green vest tops?'

'Maybe,' I teased. 'I guess you'll have to come along to find out.' Play things right and he'd also get to discover what I wore beneath it. Mentally, I began picking out my best underwear. Of course, if Victor was going to be joining us, I'd have to warn Nathan in advance. He'd been a bit off since Wednesday night, but as he'd never had any problems with me playing with other guys before, I'd largely put that down to his plans being disrupted, rather than suspicions about what I'd done after he'd left.

'I don't know. It's not really my scene.'

The first time I'd taken part, I hadn't anticipated it being my scene either. Determined not to let him off the hook – he might not make another offer, and so far he hadn't suggested an alternative date – I rambled on for a few more minutes, trying to persuade him to come along, and giving him directions to the site. The grounds were in an area of private woodland, a mile or two outside of town. Nathan knew the site owners. He even refereed for them occasionally, hence on nights like tonight we got the place to ourselves.

'How many guys, Lyssa?'

'I'm not sure. Some of them bunk off home early.' His soft cough told me I'd missed his meaning.

'How many do you play late with?'

It wasn't as if I was admitting to anything he didn't already know, but I still put off giving an answer until the silence between us grew awkward. 'Five – but only three of them will be along tonight.' David and Sam avoided the out-of-doors, and they only ever really watched anyway.

'Uh-huh.' Disappointment threaded the two syllables. His disapproval cut me up. I wanted him, you see, and I'd convinced myself it wasn't the fact I was involved with several other guys that had put him off the other night. 'It's just I'm not altogether sure I want to be number six.'

I refrained from swearing, but only just. 'Then why did you phone?' I hung up.

I'd heard it all before, about how I was a slut with extra-loose morals and a slack pussy, about how I was a user and whore. I'd taken it from former friends and strangers, but I wasn't going to listen to it again from him. Since he'd known there were other men in my life, why the hell had he even bothered to call?

He probably thought he was the guy who could save

me. That he'd fill me up with his magical dick and then I'd never need anyone else in my hoo-hah. Well, I didn't believe in magic dicks, and my pussy liked being kissed by multiple men.

I switched my phone over to aeroplane mode and shoved it deep into my pocket.

Hattie joined me about two seconds later, carrying a box of assorted greetings cards. 'I thought we could have a bit of a swap around.' I didn't hide my irritation quickly enough, causing her to frown. 'Is everything all right? Nothing's up with you and Nathan, is there? That's who you were talking to, right?'

'Nothing's wrong. We were just sorting out arrangements for tonight.' I hated lying to her; really I did, but it was easier and less risky than presenting the truth.

'Again. You're always out. He must really love you, Lyssa. He's always taking you places. Hey, you never told me what he got you for your birthday?'

'Ah, yes. It was just some bits and bobs I asked for.' In fact, he'd bought me fishnets, a garter and a whip, and suggested a bit of role-playing one night. I was to be a wannabe cabaret star, and he'd be the club manager, with whoever else wanted to join in acting as club patrons. It wasn't clear to me where the whip came in. I suspected he'd bought it to use on me, rather than the other way around.

'No fun for me tonight,' Hattie complained. 'Not that there's anyone offering to take me anywhere.'

'How come? You're in now. You can't be down for the late as well.'

'Val wanted the time off to go to her cousin's wedding reception. I'm the saint that volunteered to cover for her.' That was Hattie, always the one to help out, even if it inconvenienced herself. 'There is a plus side. I'm not wholly selfless.'

There was never a plus side to working the late shift on a Friday night. It was the worst shift of the week. Nevertheless, I waited to hear the supposed positive.

'It means I'll be around when you-know-who gets off for the night.'

And like that Leif Haralsson slipped back into the conversation. 'Wonderful,' I agreed, refusing to dampen Hattie's romantic dream. 'You can totally use that time to charm his socks off.'

'Maybe.' Hattie gave a girlish chuckle, and then she sashayed around the edge of the card rack performing her best sexy wiggle. To give her credit, it was a pretty fantastic wiggle. 'Although,' she mused, 'I'd rather charm something else off him.'

'Hattie!'

'What?' She pressed her lips together, trying to look innocent despite an enormous smirk. 'Maybe, I'll even tell you about it afterwards.'

I grinned too. Not because I believed for a second that she'd even speak to the guy, let alone get him anywhere near a bedroom, but because Hattie deserved some fun. 'Girl,' I sighed. 'If anything happens, you'd better spill, because I'm totally going to want to hear about it.'

Nathan picked me up at eight that night. He was sizzling in his night-time camos, and I could tell he was up for some serious fun. 'Careful,' I warned him. 'If you keep turning up in all these costumes, I might forget what you normally dress like.'

'Wait until you see the pimpy suit I've bought. Cabaret night is going to be mega hot. I was thinking of arranging it for next weekend. What do you think?'

'Maybe. Let's not decide yet.' I still wasn't sure about it. It sounded a little too sleazy for my tastes, although Nathan was clearly well into the idea. 'You know I don't dance, don't you, before you go getting any ideas about me cavorting with a chair, or any other nonsense.'

I guessed from his pout that was exactly what he'd been envisaging. Sadly, I was no Liza Minnelli, and definitely no Dita Von Teese.

'You'd put on a little show for me though, wouldn't you, Lys?'

'No,' I insisted. 'I don't dance.'

. We completed the first half of the journey through the evening traffic listening to the radio. It was only once we'd crossed from the suburbs out into the open countryside that we spoke again.

'You're moping,' Nathan observed, though how he could tell I wasn't sure. I'd been making a particular effort to not think about Victor or our earlier phone call. It only made my blood boil.

'Want to tell me what about?'

'Nope.'

'Something at work?'

'I said nope.'

'Has that jerk phoned you?'

An enormous telling sigh, wormed its way out of my mouth. 'Once.' It was almost a relief to admit it, even though I was loath to discuss the ins and outs of the conversation. 'Nothing of interest was said.' A fact I remained disappointed by. Maybe Victor was a jerk, but he was a jerk who hit my pleasure centres like nuclear fuel. I'd had high hopes when he'd rung.

'What the fuck were you thinking even giving him your number? When did you give him your number? Didn't you notice the fact that he had fucking weirdo stamped across his forehead? You don't give out personal information to guys like that.'

When Nathan ranted, he sounded exactly like my father, and if I'd taken his advice, the only men I'd ever have seen would have been the local vicar and the dentist.

'I mean, come on, Lys. Who the hell hangs around to watch when they've just stumbled upon some folks having a good time? The decent thing to do would be to turn a blind eye, not ogle them.'

I defensively squished my hands between my thighs. All things considered, Victor probably only weighed up at five per cent weird, versus ninety-five per cent hot. As ratios went, that wasn't a bad one. Shame then, that he'd been unable to accept the small things that were weird about me.

'I didn't actually. Sam did. And it's irrelevant anyhow.' We weren't going to see each other again.

'I suppose I ought to ask what happened after I left. He was still in the room, wasn't he?'

'Nothing,' I mumbled. I felt no inclination whatsoever to share the details of what I'd done. It'd only lead to another lecture about not placing myself in danger and being especially wary of dark, handsome strangers. Nathan seemed to have forgotten that we'd met in a taxi rank, and bonked in the back of a cab only a few minutes later.

'Really, nothing? Because Sam said you came down from the green room with him looking pretty cosy.'

'Leave it will you, Nathan,' I barked in irritation. 'Nothing happened. He didn't touch me. I've told you that already. We've had one conversation since. There won't be anymore. If you want a reason for why I'm pissed off, why don't you ask me how my birthday treat panned out? What was it I was promised – a night to remember? Yeah, I don't think I'm ever going to forget being walked in on.' I wasn't being fair, but his prodding had made me tetchy. I just wanted him to drop the subject.

Shock, then sin widened his tawny eyes. 'Shit, Lyssa! That was hardly my fault. See if I don't make it up to you tonight. Hell, I can stop the car now and make amends, if you want.'

I didn't want. A quickie in the backseat, parked up in a lay-by, wasn't going to improve my mood. Thankfully, the road was so narrow and winding, that stopping was out of the question.

'What did he phone you for?' Nathan asked, after we'd travelled another half a mile.

'A date.'

'A what?'

He hit the accelerator in his surprise, throwing us both against our seats. Thank God, it wasn't milking time at the local farm, because if there'd been anything in the road we'd have hit it. As it was we overshot the site entrance.

'Nathan!'

He stepped hard on the brake, thus bringing us to a screeching halt just past the turning. It was marked with an arrow, but I'd learned to recognise it by the two stone pillars that stood either side of the driveway. They were crumbling beneath a dressing of ivy, and I suspect mourned the days when they were grand gateposts to some country estate.

Unapologetically, Nathan put the car into reverse and swung the car around. 'And?' he enquired, once we were safely headed in the right direction.

'And nothing. I've already told you I won't be seeing him again.'

'You've said it, but I don't quite believe you. You're hot for him; I can hear it in your voice. So why aren't you seeing him again? Not because of me, I'll bet.'

'We're not together like that,' I replied, adding a defensive huff. I didn't appreciate how guilt-ridden he seemed intent on making me feel about this.

'No. No, I've got it.' Nathan gave a low whistle. 'You told him that you're already shagging three other guys, didn't you?'

I hadn't quite put it like that, but nor had I told any lies.

Nathan's mirth exploded more fully, until he was almost choking on his laughter. If he hadn't been driving, I swear I'd have clobbered him. 'What!' he laughed. 'Did you honestly think he was going to accept that? Jump right into the mix and agree to only having you on Tuesdays and Thursdays?'

'It's what you and the other guys do.'

'No, Lyssa, it isn't. We're mates. We've all known each other forever, and we all know the score. Everyone understands what the boundaries are, and the guys let me know about any wacky plans they have. Victor would never agree to that.'

I actually found it hard to fault Victor for that fact. Whenever Nathan summarised what was going on between us, he had this knack of making it sound sordid, and somehow exploitative. The reality wasn't like that, but ... Well, I guess it was just something about his tone, and the fact he made me sound like a convenience. I was just a nice simple way for them all to get their rocks off without having to moderate their behaviour in order to preserve a relationship. Well, for their information I'd have liked it if they had treated me like a proper date once in a while. And it might even have been nice to have them squabble over me, because, yes, while I loved sex – upside down, back to front, even standing on my head – that didn't mean I didn't crave a bit of old-fashioned affection from time to time. And it certainly didn't mean I warranted any less respect than they'd give a proper girlfriend.

'I suggest you shut up now, unless you want to turn round and take me home,' I warned.

My expression must have been grim, for he promptly agreed.

'I'm sorry, Lyssa. Laughing was unnecessary, but you should have realised things would never work out with him.'

I turned away from Nathan to watch the last of the scenery roll by. We'd entered the woodland now, and even the road was furrowed by tree roots. Maybe Nathan was speaking the truth, but that didn't mean he had to labour the point.

When we reached the end of the track, we found a small group of guys and girls already assembled outside the base camp lodge. Most of them were dressed like Nathan in some form of camouflage. All of them were toting laser guns. Some were busy pulling on goggles and sensors.

Nathan reached across the gearstick once he'd stopped the car engine, and squeezed my thigh. 'Forget him, Lys. Let's not argue, and just have a good time.'

'Sure.' I got out of the car determined to do as he suggested. Victor meant nothing. The most sensible thing I could do was to write him off as a one-night stand. It wasn't as if that was a new experience and hence something to dwell on.

The minute I got out of the car, my mood immediately improved. Two pairs of arms surrounded me, and I was lifted off my feet.

'Happy Birthday.'

'Happy Birthday.'

'Sorry we missed it.'

Anthony and Aaron, identical down to the last detail sandwiched me between their fit male bodies. They were both dressed head to foot in soft form-fitting black clothing that I wriggled against. Anthony smelled of cologne and citrus shower gel. His brother cheekily dropped a kiss onto the end of my nose, before he restored me to terra firma. 'Are you going to run with us? You know we'll keep you safe.' They each gave me sly nudges.

'What if I don't want to be safe?' I asked archly.

'Then I'm happy to play the big bad wolf.' Aaron howled.

His brother clapped him on the shoulder. 'Wolves,' he insisted. 'And may I say, Lyssa, that you look particularly edible in that outfit.'

# Chapter Three

No question, the twins were good for my self-esteem. Two hours later, I'd almost, but not quite, forgotten about Victor. By then I was pumped up on adrenaline and endorphins, having crawled through countless bushes, and having zapped my way to victory, along with the twins, in the first game. Now that the twilight was deepening, and the number of players had dwindled down to a handful, we were all actively hunting each other.

Victor was just a blip in my past, a bit of fun that wasn't meant to be repeated and certainly nothing to be solemn about. More importantly, he definitely wasn't a reason to miss out on the abundance of hunky male flesh on offer in the woods tonight. Fun with three guys totally outweighed fun with just Victor, no matter how hot and intriguing I'd found him. And that wasn't being greedy, it was simply being honest.

It was as I sneaked along the base of a rocky outcropping that I spotted the twins. Aaron was crouched behind a shrub on the left, while Anthony stood poised with his back to the trunk of a massive oak. No doubt they'd seen me too, and given that they were both faster and stronger, they were probably waiting for me to drop my gun, put my hands in the air and surrender. I was under no illusions about the fact that if I tried to break cover, they'd both be on me in seconds. My boys were like two leopards on the prowl. Not that being captured by them would be in any way a bad thing. Imagine what they might do, two sexy as hell blonds, identical down to the finest detail. Hell, my body zinged with the sheer anticipation of it. Maybe one would play look-out while the other got to grips with me, and then they'd swap over. Perhaps, if I was really lucky, they'd both interrogate me together.

As it was, my capture came not from the fore, but the rear. I didn't even hear Nathan until he was on me. The bleep of my sensor signalled I'd been hit a millisecond before Nathan's muscular arms wrapped around my waist and he lifted me clean off my feet.

'Got you,' his gruff purr whispered into my ear, making my insides heat even as I jumped in surprise. 'Now, are you going to come quietly, or am I going to have to restrain you?'

Nathan had to be at least 180 pounds of solid muscle, more than enough to pick me up and run with me at much the same pace as he did with a rugby ball. Restraining me would take zero effort on his part. He had only to close one of his big hands around my wrists like that, and I was his to do with as he pleased.

'I kind of get the feeling you've been avoiding me.'

That wasn't actually true. I'd been annoyed with him earlier in the evening, but I'd since run off that tetchiness. It was purely by fluke that our paths hadn't crossed.

'You've just not been very good at finding me.' I pushed back against Nathan's hold, bringing our bodies into close contact. He felt so warm, and we fitted together so perfectly, it didn't make sense to push him away. It wasn't fair to blame Nathan for Victor's faults, and besides, he'd promised me some fun. And, I really did love the way he smelled when he got all hot and agitated.

'Yes.' Nathan made an appreciative groan right into my ear. He might have only had hold of me for a second or two, but his erection was already a stiff brand against my bum. 'So, are you going to come quietly?'

'Huh! I never come quietly.'

If we'd been in an action movie, I'd have unleashed a fantastic special move at this junction that would have put Nathan flat on his back despite his height and weight advantage. Sadly, I hadn't been ninja trained. Mind you, the ground didn't look all that soft, and one of the great joys of Nathan's strength was the ease with which he picked me up. It made having sex upright, instead of scrabbling around in the dirt, a definite option.

I sensed his mirth as his lips brushed my shoulder, and then the pulse point in my neck. 'You scream like a goddamned banshee most of the time,' he muttered. 'That's not a complaint.' He snuggled closer, and pushed a hand under my top. Subtle, he wasn't. Regardless, the moment his fingers tightened around my nipple, I was aching for what came next.

'Babe, you have too many clothes on,' he grumbled, and plucked at the waistband of my trousers. 'You know we're going to have to do something about that. My God.' He feigned shock. 'You even have panties on.'

'Well, you know it wasn't my idea to play laser tag tonight. We could have gone skinny dipping instead.'

'Yeah, I bet you'd have liked that. I know what a lech you are when there's a bit of male flesh around to ogle.' He laughed, and then nibbled the junction between my ear and neck. 'The thing is, Lyssa. I like seeing you get a bit sweaty, and a bit out of breath. And I definitely like catching you when you're all warm. It's much nicer than cold and wet.' He nuzzled a bit closer, now in possession of both my breasts. 'And you know the thing about nakedness, is while it might be convenient it's just not half as sexy as seeing you with your trousers and those itty-bitty panties you wear dangling around your thighs.' Immediately, he traced one palm down over my stomach to where my belt buckle sat.

I let his fingertips wander a moment, and then clamped

a hand down on top of his to prevent him undressing me right away. Instead, I held his hand captive as I turned so that we were facing.

Nathan's eyes were wide as saucers, his generous mouth open, betraying the excited hitch to his breathing. Like me, he was fired up. The long wedge of his erection showed clearly beneath his night-time camos. 'Lys,' he begged, leaning forward to kiss me. The brush of his lips brought additional fire to my insides. My pulse fluttered wildly. 'I don't even want to think about doing without you. Promise me you won't go getting any more strange ideas about groping other men.'

I took that request with a grain of salt. He knew perfectly well that the twins were close by, and wouldn't stand back forever, and I wouldn't stop them joining in the minute they chose to do so.

I let him undo my belt, while we kissed, but stopped him from doing any more by dropping his trousers. I wanted to touch him, to feel his need building and know he wanted me. Just because Victor didn't appreciate what I had to offer, didn't mean other guys felt the same way.

Nathan's shaft filled my palm. I broke off our kiss in order to bow my head against his broad chest and look down at what I held. The waist of his trousers was stretched taut around his hips, but dipped lower at the front, where I'd freed him from the confines of his clothes. He was hard all right; his rosy tip peeped up from between the ring of my fingers.

One of my favourite times I'd spent with Nathan was when he and the twins had come over so that I could compare them. They'd sat side by side on my sofa with their jeans dropped, and I'd watched the three of them jerk themselves to fullness. A detailed comparison had taken me the rest of the night. I'd touched, and sucked, and then after the twins had gone home, Nathan had taken me over the coffee table until I was senseless, and I'd told him just how eager I was to have his mates do the same. Wonder that he was, he'd called them back immediately. We'd been enjoying similar dates ever since.

No longer content with stroking Nathan, with one fingertip I made a slippery circle right around the head of his erection.

'Babe!' A groan rolled up his throat. A glance upward told me his eyes were closed.

Feeling wicked, I dipped my head a fraction further, while I also wrestled his pants right down to his knees. The leaf litter crunched beneath us as I sank to the task.

'Don't suck me,' Nathan insisted, catching me beneath my arms. 'I'm too on edge. I can't handle that thing you do with your tongue.'

'What thing?' If his words weren't code for 'suck me, please, and do it right now' then I knew nothing about men and even less about Nathan. 'Oh, you mean this thing.' Eight nights ago I'd sucked him off. I'd tied him to a chair in his dining room and made him wait for a change. No going first that night. He'd had to watch me entertain the twins before I took pity and went down on him. I'd barely got my mouth around him before he'd started bucking and making one hell of a noise. It wasn't much different now. His knees nearly buckled when I landed my first kiss near the base of his cock. The slow climb to the tip had him ripping the band out of my hair and then tying the blonde strands in knots around his fingers. By the time I reached my goal, and actually wrapped my lips around him, he was so stiff I had to strain to reach him.

'You're not going to come already, are you?'

The question earned me a groan.

I gave him another naughty lick. He tasted good, a fragrant mix of spicy and tart, so I couldn't resist repeating the action, tasting him over and over in the way he swore he couldn't take. He did take it though. I moved with the roll of his hips, letting him dictate our motion. Not for long though, as he was weeping copiously.

'Lyssa. Get up here, girl.' He grabbed hold of me and virtually lifted me from my knees into his arms. I obligingly wrapped my thighs around his waist. If I'd been wearing a skirt, he'd have been straight in me. Instead, we had to negotiate several excruciating seconds of him trying to find my zip.

'Put me down, Nathan.'

He watched, his swooping brows drawn together, as I stepped out of my trousers. His breath was coming hard now, and his hands kneaded the sides of his thighs. 'Knickers too,' he prompted. We were surrounded by acres of woodland; no one was going to see, leastways, nobody who wasn't here with that express purpose in mind.

Regardless, I shook my head. 'Ah, come on, this itty little bit of fabric ain't going to stop you,' I teased. It might slow him down a fraction though, until he got himself appropriately dressed.

'Damn!' His teeth drove a ridge into his lower lip. Ten seconds, I reckoned, from the moment he dug the condom out of his pocket to the point where he'd sheathed himself, then his hands were on me again.

Nathan didn't pick me up, not straight away, even though he was clearly desperate to bury himself deep. Instead, he pushed his hand inside the triangle of cloth covering my mound. Three fingers stroked along the seam of my sex, the middle one dipped into the pool of wet heat gathered there, making me want to screech. Hell, if he just kept me here, trapped against the tree trunk, doing that, I'd be seeing stars in minutes. All he needed to do was … If he'd just move his finger a little so that …

Instead, he moved us closer together, so that not even the night breeze could squeeze between us.

The smell of his skin mingled with the scent of my growing arousal. My body was working with the motion of his hand now, riding and sliding; my clit growing harder with each precious stroke.

'Lyssa.'

He lifted me one-handed, as if I only weighed an ounce, when in truth I was pretty darn curvy. He didn't even brace me against the tree for support, just held me against his chest, so I could feel the drum of his heart behind the solid slabs of muscle. Meanwhile, the fingers of his other hand never stopped working. They stayed inside my knickers, riding back and forth over my clit, reminding me why, despite our disparate politics, and general lack of any commonality besides sex, we got on so well.

Nathan liked me eager and, more importantly, wet, something the dance of his fingertips had no trouble achieving. The moment he thought I was ready, his erection was there, bucking up against my entrance, eager to say a grand hello.

He'd sheath himself deep. He always did. Nathan liked doing it upright for that very reason. He loved the way gravity tugged me down onto him.

'Do it,' I encouraged.

Surprisingly, he held back. 'What if I don't? What if I string this out because I'm enraged that you've been prioritising some other guy over me?' He raised an eyebrow to give his words emphasis, and somehow I knew he was serious. It didn't matter to him that I regularly had two other guys beside him, but the fact that I might have given myself to Victor without his approval really riled him.

'Don't. He's not important, Nathan.'

'He'd better not be. Still ...'

'Please,' I begged. 'You know the twins are close by. You wouldn't want them thinking you weren't up to it. They might choose to step in.'

'Those two –' he gave an irritated snort '– like they're ever going to give you what you really want.'

'Will.'

'Won't,' he laughed.

But then nor would Nathan, not that I said so. There was no point in rocking the boat so directly when we were getting on so well. 'Well, I don't see what's wrong with wanting a matching pair?' I said, steering the topic away from Victor.

Nathan just shook his head. 'Nothing, if it's a pair of socks. They're brothers, Lys. I mean ewww! They're totally not into each other. You've no chance of them having you together.'

At least he was aware of what I wanted, even if he had no intention of providing it. As for the twins, Nathan was right, but only on a point of technicality. The twins were happy to play together, but ask them to touch one another ... No. Way. They got weird about even shaking one another's hands. They were even worse than Nathan was about ensuring no guy–guy contact occurred.

I nipped the skin of his neck. 'If I asked, you'd share me with another guy though, wouldn't you?'

Irritation rumbled through his chest. 'Is that what you think this Victor guy is going to give you?'

'No.'

'Babe, you know I'm not into guys. We've been over this. I don't mind sharing, just as long as there's no overstepping the boundaries, and there's plenty of you and me doing what comes natural.' He rocked into me, just to prove that point. And boy, it did feel good. Really, really, ridiculously good. I absolutely liked doing what came natural too, and had every intention of doing it multiple times tonight; with Nathan, and with Anthony, and Aaron, and whoever damn well else was still around if they were up for it. Damn Victor and his stipulations. I didn't need anything beyond what I'd already got. And what I had was good, as attested to by the heavy pulse in my womb.

Nathan blew out a steamy breath. 'That's right; you just sink down onto me.' He drew back, before slipping into me slowly again, smooth and steady. I was no sylph, but Nathan held on to me as though there were no acrobatics involved, as though he were stood in the open massaging himself with his fist, and not sliding repeatedly into me. 'Another bloke would just get in the way, babe. You can see that, can't you? Imagine all those extra limbs making things awkward. We'd have to signal pace changes.'

Without such a warning, he switched things up a gear, so that he hammered forward into me, lifting me a fraction higher with each thrust. Still, even his extra effort couldn't entirely persuade me to his point of view. I found it all too easy to imagine another guy, or two, present, but then the possibility of being loved like that filled more of my waking thoughts than was probably healthy.

'You've got it good, Lys. Don't start getting greedy.'

This wasn't about numbers. It was about an itch I needed to scratch. Maybe once would be enough, but I'd never know until I'd tried it.

'You know he wouldn't have to touch you, Nathan. I'd be in the middle.' If we travelled forward using baby steps, it might give him the requisite time to adjust to the notion.

'Lys.' He slowed the jerk of his hips a fraction. 'I swear if you mention that man's name again tonight, I'll ...'

OK. I knew when to back off. 'I wasn't thinking about him. You're totally right. I don't need another man, just the one I have.' I squeezed him tight with my inner muscles, eliciting a glorious grunt from him, and a moan from me. He picked up our previous pace again, even built on it a little. 'After all, you can do me both ways at once, can't you, baby.'

So, bad me, I hadn't entirely let the issue go.

Nathan had the grace to chuckle. 'God, you're so dirty. Is that what this is about – you want it back there too?'

Without waiting for a reply, he thrust his hand under the string of my thong.

My grip tightened fast around his shoulders as he sought his new goal. That was it. That was where I needed his touch – circling and brushing insistently against the tight little furl of muscle. 'Go on, push them in,' I encouraged.

He had to slow our movement right down, but he did it. Nathan wetted his fingers, then one … two digits slipped into my rear. He kept them stiff, so I could ride up and down on them as we resumed our former punchy rhythm. It wasn't subtle, but bugger subtle. My body sucked at both his fingers and his erection. I'd take my satisfaction anyway I could get it, and this was sure to make my climax crackle with extra vigour.

'Lys. Lys. Ah, babe. That is so right. Squeeze me. Oh, God. Yes.'

I closed my eyes and imagined a second pair of hands cradling my bottom, and that instead of Nathan's fingers, it was a second man spearing into me from behind.

One of the things I loved was when all the men I knew closed in around me. I loved the weight of the bodies, the musk of their skin, and just the general pleasure of being tightly cocooned. The obvious next step for me was to have full-on sex with them like that, but so far it hadn't happened. I dreamed of basking in the cacophony of their heartbeats as they thudded in unison and we all ground together. It'd feel wonderful to have them inside me together.

It was while focussed on that thought that my orgasm crept up. It started in my rump with my muscles clamping tight around Nathan's fingers. Then built; zapped across to my clit, where it seemed to find extra strength.

Sweat beaded across Nathan's back. Damn! Was he racing me? He always liked to be first. But this felt like he was striving for Olympic glory, not shagging me senseless up against a tree. As if it mattered who reached the finish first. It wasn't as if there were medals at stake, or there was a scoreboard. Though the notion had possibilities for a future night – Sexual Gymnastics. What would an upright shag warrant? Maybe a 6.2 difficulty, and then it'd be up to the judges regarding the execution.

Nathan shifted his stance and the concept of winners and losers became irrelevant. Not a damn thing mattered anymore. The world was drawn in tight. For a fraction of a second my whole body seemed to stretch towards a bright spot of light on the horizon. Then I was being bounced and battered, being pulled apart and remade.

I threw my head back and my release flowed out of me along with my voice. I'd be hoarse tomorrow, but who cared. Coming like this was worth a little discomfort.

It was barely over, my body still twitching with the

aftershocks, when I was manhandled out of Nathan's arms and lowered onto a patch of grass. Aaron's wiry frame immediately towered over me. He'd stripped, so that he was clothed only in the dappled shadows of the leaves. Down he sank, between my splayed thighs. The heat of his mouth met my plump, wet sex, which immediately fanned the embers of my orgasm back to life.

Nathan had torn off the condom; now his hand slid in a punishing rhythm up and down his shaft. He shuffled over to where Aaron had placed me, and dipped down to my level. There was no need to ask what he wanted. His eyes were misty. God, he was close. The moment my mouth sealed around his shaft that was it. He came in long shuddering jets.

Spent, Nathan sat back on his haunches. He watched as Aaron's twin straddled my waist. Anthony too was naked, and took no time in relieving me of my T-shirt and bra. Anthony had a thing about getting me naked, especially from the waist up. Actually, I suspected he had a bit of a breast fetish.

'Lys,' he sighed as he squeezed my breasts together around his length. 'These are so gorgeous. You don't mind if I just borrow them for a little bit.' Considering the wonderful sucks his brother was giving to my clit, I had no breath to reply either way. I suppose given a better angle, I might have licked him when his cock crested the valley of my breasts in order to indicate my consent.

'Hey, go easy on her there a bit, mate. Not so rough.' Nathan had finished cleaning himself up. He bent back down and took possession of my mouth again, this time ravaging me with lips and tongue. 'Just tell me if these two beasts aren't doing you right, and I'll have them replaced.'

I didn't want them replaced. They were perfect. The twins always were. The only thing he could do to improve the moment, would be to suddenly lose his inhibitions about gay sex and move his slowly reviving erection into Anthony's mouth, or better still, kneel down behind Aaron – who was still loving my clit – and take him from behind.

I knew better than to hope it'd actually happen. To date, I'd only seen guys fuck on film. In the future, I absolutely intended to see it up close and personal. And if the current company weren't prepared to oblige me on that, well, then, I'd just have to look elsewhere.

My attention wandered to the surrounding woodland at that moment, perhaps thinking I might spot an obliging, randy satyr lurking nearby.

Such a figure was closer than I could ever have anticipated.

'Victor!' I squealed, as my climax exploded.

# Chapter Four

Why was he here? How long had he stood there? His black clothing made him virtually impossible to see, particularly as he was taking care not to draw attention. I saw him though. I saw the pale lanterns that were his eyes; the hard, urgent lust reflected in them, not to mention the tent pole in his trousers that he was struggling not to rub.

'I'm not sure I want to be number six,' he'd said. I'd taken that to mean we were over, that he wanted exclusivity, and yet, here he was, watching me with three other guys and clearly aroused by my antics. Maybe I'd misinterpreted him. Perhaps, I'd been hasty in hanging up.

Around me, Anthony, then Aaron and finally Nathan reached orgasm. They hunched around me, each holding me close while somehow managing to avoid each other. 'I'm getting cold,' I complained, and gently pushed them away. For once, I wasn't interested in extended cuddles.

59

I needed to catch up with Victor and speak to him. 'I'm going to head back to the shack for a brew.'

'Wait up, Lys. We'll all go back. It's lock up time anyway.' Aaron flipped himself onto his feet. He rooted under a pile of leaves and found his clothes. A second or two later, his brother followed suit.

In that time, Victor had slipped away, assuming he'd actually been there, and my eyes weren't playing tricks on me.

Once dressed, I dug my phone out of my pocket and switched it on. I had twelve missed call messages, all from the same number. Victor had also sent me a text message.

I didn't mean what you seem to think I did. I don't want what they want.
We need to talk.
Victor.

Not wanting what they – presumably my other lovers – wanted could be interpreted in a myriad of different ways, everything from 'I just want to watch' to 'drop them all, you and I are meant to be together'. OK, so I agreed. We did need to talk, even if only to clear up what exactly it was he wanted.

'I could get pissed off,' Nathan came up behind me to whisper in my ear as I was still bent over my phone.

I hastily closed the message. 'Why?'

He raised both brows, as if stunned that I didn't know. 'It's really not cool to scream another guy's name when you come. Especially when you already have three to choose from.'

I turned to face him, and found he'd dressed again. He was right, of course. It was rude, but I hadn't intended it. It was only that Victor had startled me.

'I thought you were done with him. It's what you said earlier.'

'He was here,' I explained. My gaze strayed to the tree he'd been concealed against. 'I was looking right at him.'

Nathan eyed me sceptically. He followed my line of sight, and on discovering nothing, turned a slow three hundred and sixty degrees without spotting a single bit of evidence to support my claim.

'He's gone now.'

'Evidently.'

Nathan didn't believe me; hence we began the trek back to base camp in awkward silence. Every crunch of leaf and twig beneath our feet sounded especially loud. Without conscious planning, the guys formed a wall of muscle around me, making it hard for me to look for Victor amongst the trees. Instead, I had a view of guns and chests.

'Did either of you see a bloke watching us?' Nathan asked the twins, confirming my suspicion that he thought I was lying.

Anthony shook his head. His blond hair was full of leaves, so I reached up to brush them out.

'My eyes were on Lyssa,' Aaron muttered, watching me comb the foliage from his brother's hair. 'Was there one?'

'Lyssa seems to think so.'

I didn't think so. I knew so. Victor had definitely been watching us, or leastways, he'd been watching me.

'Weird,' said Aaron. 'Did you recognise him?'

'It was a weirdo from Wednesday night,' Nathan replied, before I'd even opened my mouth. 'He's creepy. I'm wondering how the hell he knew we'd be here.'

'The bloke at the gallery?' Aaron dug in trouser pocket for his phone. 'Yeah, I remember. David texted me something about that. Said he burst in on you and demanded he be allowed to join in.'

'That's not what happened,' I snarled. Irritated by the remark. 'Firstly, Victor didn't burst in on us. And secondly, he didn't demand anything of anyone.' He'd actually been very polite. 'As for how he found us, I told him we'd be here. I did say I'd spoken to him earlier.'

'Aye,' Nathan drawled incredulously, 'but you said you wouldn't be hearing from him again, not that you'd invited him along.' He swiped at one of the overhanging tree branches, which flicked back narrowly avoiding striking Anthony in the face.

'What harm is he doing if he's just watching?' Anthony caught the branch and gingerly held it out of the way.

Both his brother and Nathan glared at him.

'Hey, I was just saying.'

'He's freaky.' Nathan started twitching his finger over his laser pistol like he was itching to use it. 'That and what's to say it'll stop at watching. God knows what sort of perversion he's capable of. I, for one, don't like him, and I certainly don't appreciate him ogling my arse.'

And wasn't that likely the heart of the problem. God forbid anyone did anything so gay as look at another fellow's arse. Not that I thought Victor was even vaguely interested in Nathan's bottom. No, if he was interested in anyone's bottom it was mine. That's why he'd phoned me, and not Nathan.

'Well, I'm going to talk to him if he's still around,' I said.

'Don't!'

OK, so I'm fairly placid normally, but Nathan's tone needed addressing. I grabbed hold of his sleeve in order to bring him to a halt. 'Pardon?' Who the hell did he think he was, ordering me around like that? 'You don't get to dictate my actions, Nathan Lowell. If Victor's come all this way to see me, then the least I can do is say hello and find out why.'

'You're not doing yourself or us any favours by doing so. He's just going to see it as encouragement, when you ought to be sending the opposite message to this guy. We don't need another man muscling in on things.'

'Don't we? You might not think so, but I think, the more the merrier.' I didn't specifically. The current arrangement suited fine. That wasn't really the issue though. 'I don't recall you having a problem with inviting any of your mates to join us.'

'That's different,' Nathan huffed, refusing to look at me. 'They are my mates. He's ... he's not anybody. He's not going to get it.'

What exactly, I wondered, was there to get?

Nathan remained twenty steps ahead of me the rest of the way back. The twins were contemplative. I couldn't fathom Nathan's anger. It didn't make any logical sense. Why should his reaction to Victor be any different to what he felt about Anthony or Aaron for example? What was it about Victor that made Nathan so darn pissy? Yes, he was massively homophobic, but that couldn't really be it. It wasn't as if Victor had come on to him. He'd only ever seemed interested in me. As for the whole 'he's not my friend' thing, that was plain juvenile.

'Fuck!' he bellowed as we exited the woods. There was no need to guess the cause of his outburst. True to expectations, there was no fire, no major casualty, and no evidence of theft, only a lone, dark figure sat on a bench outside the cabin.

'Victor!' Maybe it was a reaction to Nathan's griping, but jubilation welled inside me on seeing him. He looked stunning. Jet black suited him even more than it did the twins. His clothes clung to his body, emphasising his lean, toned physique, while the glow from the overhead security light warmed his skin tone, and added an additional sheen to his silky black hair. However, my joy was quickly followed by an equally emotive sinking feeling, when I realised Nathan was charging straight for him, and I wasn't going to be able to get between them in time.

'Stop! Nathan, wait.' Some girls like the idea of guys having punch-ups over them, I'm not among them. I'd much rather everyone got along. The thought of either of them getting hurt made me jumpy as hell, and if there was blood involved, I'd faint.

Victor was on his feet by the time Nathan reached him.

'What are you, some kind of deviant?' Nathan's fists clenched tight by his sides, but to my immense relief, he didn't take a swing.

'No more than you.'

'You told her that you weren't interested. Hang on, what did you just say?'

'Shush, Nathan.' I pushed my way in front of him, and crossed to Victor. 'It's good to see you.' I pressed a kiss to his cheek.

Nathan's eyebrows shot up into his hairline. He wasn't happy, but that was no excuse for him behaving like a baboon. I was sure that given a sensible conversation, we could sort things out. The twins tactfully chose to stay out of it. They gathered up the laser tag equipment and disappeared into the cabin to pack it away.

'That's not actually what I said,' Victor insisted, answering Nathan's claim, though he was looking at me. 'Lyssa, I never said I wasn't interested.' Disappointment shadowed his silver-grey eyes.

How could I have forgotten those eyes? I thought his image had been burned into my brain, but I'd only remembered his overall composition without recalling the brilliance of the individual details. For good or bad, I lapped up the sight of him again now; his hair, his eyes, even the hewn rigid planes of his face.

'I'm glad to hear it.'

Victor's smile told me he was pleased I understood. Only Nathan seemed to have a problem with our reconciliation. 'Christ!' His bellow exploded from his mouth like a gunshot. 'Hell if I'm sticking around to watch you go doe-eyed over him.' He turned his back and trotted down the veranda steps. 'Call me in the week if you're not too busy. You can hitch a ride home with Aaron, that's assuming you're sane enough not to accept a lift from a stranger.'

Wow. He really was in a one. He flicked the switch on his key fob, so that his car lights blinked on, bathing us all in unflatteringly bright light. A moment later, Nathan swung his car into reverse, creating a spray of gravel, then he swerved out of the parking lot, leaving Victor and I alone in the darkness.

'So, we've established that boyfriend number one doesn't like me.' Victor flexed each of his fingers from the death grip they'd formed around the paper coffee cup he was holding.

'He's –' I started to explain, except I didn't actual know what Nathan was so rattled about. Typically, he was the most easy-going man I knew, unless you counted his need to be constantly first. Prior to this he'd certainly never shown any signs of jealousy.

'– pissed off,' Victor helpfully suggested. 'What – does he think I'm going to carry you off to technicoloured happy-ever-after-land?'

'No,' I sighed, giving a frown. 'I don't think so. Are you?' It was difficult not to get a little excited at that possibility. What woman didn't occasionally dream of being whisked away by Prince Charming? Not that I imagined Victor to be anything so pure.

He took a swig of his coffee. 'That would involve knowing the way.' He tipped his head towards the cabin door. 'What about those two?'

'They're cool.' At least, I assumed so. The twins were bolshie enough that they'd have been out here making themselves heard if they'd had anything to say on the matter. The fact that they weren't, suggested they weren't feeling threatened.

67

'Why are you here, Victor?'

He raised his shoulders sheepishly. 'Well, you don't answer your phone, so you left me little choice.'

'You weren't interested,' I reminded him

This time when his grip tightened around the cup, the lid popped off.

'Actually, I said I wasn't interested in being at the end of a list. It's not the same thing at all.'

Oops! I stuffed my hands into my pockets, and hunched my shoulders up around my ears. 'So, what does that mean?' Rather than face him and await an answer, I spilled a few coins out of my pocket and fed them into the coffee vending machine.

Victor came up behind me as I waited for the cup to fill. He curled a strand of my hair around the tip of his index finger. For a moment he seemed entranced, until I jostled him as I scooped up my drink.

'To be honest, Lyssa, I'm not altogether sure why I'm here. Only that I knew I didn't want to leave things like that between us. I hated the idea of you thinking that I'd somehow judged you.'

Armed with a steaming cup, I steeled myself to look at him again. Victor was staring down at his toes, so that his eyelashes shadowed his face, and hid the winter light in his eyes. A faint line of stubble softened his jaw and upper lip, which made me want to reach up and touch his face. We were standing close enough that I could

68

smell his scent, a warm woodsy blend, with a base note of oriental spice that was uniquely him.

'You watched,' I said, letting him know that I'd seen him in the woods. My gaze dropped to the bulge straining his fly. I guessed that he'd hurried away the moment I'd spotted him, and thus his tension had gone unrelieved. Nothing else would explain his continued arousal. 'Is that all you want to do?' Teasingly, I reached out and brushed the top of his thigh, letting him know that I was willing.

'Lyssa,' he said in warning, but as there was no force behind it, I continued to walk my fingers towards his fly. 'Don't. Really, I can't.'

'Can't what?' First one finger, then a second landed upon the hummock made by his shaft. The fabric of his trousers strained across the bulge. 'One minute you're saying you're here for me. The next: that I'm supposed to ignore this.' I was being naughty now, but hell, naughty was my middle name, or should have been. I cupped the swell of his erection. 'You ought to know I'm a straightforward sort of girl. If you're interested, I'm definitely willing.' His breath caught as I squeezed. He was like putty – pliable, and eager. And if my strokes were expert, then Victor's responses were equally practised.

'No.' He jerked out of my grasp, as I strained upwards to possess his mouth too. He rubbed his lips, even though we hadn't touched. 'I can't.'

'Nathan doesn't get to dictate who I kiss.' I was

determined to make that particularly clear, but it didn't seem to be that which was stopping him.

'Let's just get to know one another a bit first.'

That's exactly what I'd had in mind. One learned a lot about a guy from the way he kissed. Things like whether he was considerate, or dominant. If he was too pushy or wet, he'd likely be like that in other respects too. I reached from him again, only for him to fold his hand tightly around mine. His lips bussed against my knuckles.

'I want us to be intimate, but not in that way. I can't be like your other lovers. It can't be physical between us.'

Considering the bulge he was still sporting, I was pretty certain he could.

'I want to admire you, Lyssa. Not consume you.'

Everything tumbled into place with that statement. I understood him now. 'You want to get off on watching me.'

His nostrils flared slightly. 'I'm not a voyeur.'

Oh, but he was. We'd met twice and both times he'd watched. I reminded him of that too. 'What exactly do you call it then?'

'Admiration of a beautiful woman.'

I rolled my eyes at the compliment. 'So you don't want to watch me with other men.'

His awkward squirm told me plainly what he refused to voice. That was exactly what he wanted from me.

I guess that made him feel guilty, which was why he refused to admit to it.

As a rule, I didn't believe in making things unnecessarily difficult for myself, particularly where the pursuit of pleasure was concerned. If there were no barriers to sexual congress, then why erect them. Still, I was intrigued, and maybe a little curious as to how long it would take me to corrupt him to my will. I didn't want Victor to only watch me. I wanted him to touch me. But we could work on that part.

'OK,' I agreed.

'OK?'

Really, he didn't need to act befuddled. He might be embarrassed about what he was asking for, but I was feeling tingly and amused at the thought of showing off. Plus, I reckoned he'd be in my bed before the night was out. 'Here – or should we go somewhere warmer?' It was curious that I was quite happy to touch myself for Victor's entertainment, but I balked at doing a bit of sexy wiggling to music in order to enact Nathan's cabaret fantasy.

He took a deep, slow breath. 'My studio.'

I cheerily patted his bottom. 'Then let's go.'

# Chapter Five

Victor warned me on the drive over that his studio was nothing swish. It lay on the edge of an industrial park, bordered on one side by abandoned railway tracks and another by a grubby canal. Victor occupied the top floor of a converted engine shed, accessed by a set of external iron steps, which were virtually impossible to see in the dark. The security light did come on, but only after I'd tripped and nearly broken my neck.

'I need to get someone out to alter that thing,' Victor muttered. 'It's blasted all use at the moment. It wouldn't see a cat off, let alone a burglar.'

Once inside, he flicked on rows of switches. There were no overhead lights, just a multitude of lamps and odd looking coloured lanterns that created coloured light bubbles at various spots within the room. The walls were bare brick, so too was the barrel-shaped roof. Plain boards creaked underfoot, masked in one or two places by threadbare rugs.

'As I said it's not much, but it's functional and its home.'

'You don't live here though?' The place reminded me of my granddad's garage, except with pots in place of disembowelled TVs and paint in place of car parts. The garage had been an exciting place to visit and have an adventure as a child, but it wasn't somewhere you could comfortably live, and as I'd grown older, I'd become less enamoured of the grot. Not that Victor's studio was dirty. It was just a bit haphazard in its arrangement.

'Actually, I pretty much do, though home is officially elsewhere.' He draped our coats over a bust of a tentacle-faced alien. 'So.' Victor swept his arm before him in a wide arch. 'Welcome to my domain. The bathroom is on the right, the kitchen at the back there.' By which he meant a fridge, a kettle and a sink. 'And the pottery is … Well, you can see it.'

Pottery, along with the instruments of its construction, littered virtually every surface. Animal figurines nestled between five-foot urns; strange, misshapen beasties frolicked alongside flighty nymphs, and one entire windowsill housed a row of heads. I later discovered they were toby jugs. There were soup mugs and goblets, all sorts of tableware and plant pots, hundreds of vases and numerous plates. 'Hm,' I remarked, while turning over one piece that was surely a companion piece to those currently on display at the gallery.

'I guess I won't expect any fan girl gushing,' he remarked, taking the vase off me.

'It's not very ...' I was about to say exciting, but thought better of it. Insulting his artwork wasn't going to get me into his pants.

To my astonishment, Victor began to laugh. 'It's not very ... what? Go on say what you were going to. Be truthful now.'

'It's just,' I said, squirming as I sought a way to be tactful. 'That they're a bit grey. I'm not saying that they're not good, or that you can't ... potter.' Was that the right term? 'Only that they're ... Well, they're grey.'

'Boring?' he added, arching an eyebrow.

I refused to say either way.

'It's supposed to be a study of contrasts; of dark and light.'

'Uh-huh,' I agreed, dubiously. 'Then shouldn't there be more black and white in the design?'

'My previous collection was orange. No doubt you'd have found that one too garish. I'll have to hope my current work is more to your taste.'

'What colour's that – blue?'

Thank God he had a sense of humour or I'd probably have found myself out on the street.

Victor passed me a tiny vase. The base consisted of speckled stone, but a splash of vibrant purple curved around the neck. This vase – and it was only one of a collection seated next to his modern electric kiln – teased you into turning it in order to follow the trail of colour.

'Wow – it's beautiful. I'd buy something like this.'

'No need. You can keep that one.'

'Seriously?'

He took it from me, and wrapped it in bubble wrap, securing the package with a piece of sticky tape. 'Consider it a belated birthday gift. Now, drinks?'

He headed towards the kitchenette, while I stowed the vase in my bag. When I caught up, he was fishing two obviously home-made mugs from the depths of the enormous Belfast sink. He rinsed them out while the kettle boiled. I'd been anticipating wine rather than coffee to get us in the mood, but then Victor didn't seem in any hurry to get his hands, or his eyes or whatever it was, on me.

'Black only, I'm afraid.' He shook the milk carton in confirmation. 'It's either curdled or frozen. Possibly both.'

'Black's fine.' I accepted the mug, curling my hands around its heat. I wondered if Victor would feel this warm if I pushed my hands beneath his clothing and found his skin. I longed to touch him, explore him. I had several lovers, but none of them were particularly new. Victor was like a present sat beneath a Christmas tree days before the twenty-fifth. It was all tease and temptation, because it was forbidden to unwrap it. A present I could shake though. I could explore its contours in order to determine what was inside. Victor wouldn't even let me do that.

'Shall we sit down?'

He guided me into an old-fashioned, high-backed armchair, but then remained standing, pacing back and forth. Two fingers pinched repetitively at his lips. I couldn't tell if he was fretting, or planning what came next. Even I, with my multitude of partners, sometimes found it difficult to articulate what it was I wanted, especially if it related to some special secret fantasy.

Was I Victor's secret fantasy? Perhaps it was egotistical to think that, and yet he'd sought me out in the dark, in the woods, and stolen me away from three other lovers to be with him. There had to be some reason for that.

'Victor?' I enquired. His head turned and he stopped pacing. I patted the chair arm, hoping to tempt him closer. 'Why don't you tell me what you'd like me to do?'

He formed a steeple with his fingers and tapped them against his chin. 'Why do you do it? Why so many men?'

I unlaced my boots and curled my feet up beneath me. 'It's fun.' That was the simplest and most honest answer, though if we were going to be analytical about it, I appreciated both the freedom and the boundaries the arrangement gave me. After my experience with my last boyfriend, I was done with being ordered about and made to feel guilty for my desires. My current arrangement meant no one got too close, no one tried to stamp a claim on me. It was like being single, only with more sex.

'Why, is it fun?'

'Why do you enjoying watching?' I countered. Even with someone who knew about my arrangements, I found it uncomfortable to talk about.

'Who says I do?'

I grinned. 'Isn't that why we're here? So, just tell me and I'll oblige.'

Victor paced some more. Perhaps his studio hadn't been the ideal place to come. He seemed unable to settle here. He tensed every time the wind rattled the window-panes, or a floorboard creaked. 'What if I don't want you to do anything?'

Beggar the thought! I guess my expression must have said as much.

'Do you never just hang out?'

'God, no!' Well, I suppose I did with Hattie, but not with any of my male 'friends'. When we met it was with the intention of having sex. In essence, my social life was just a long string of such dates. There wasn't much time for anything else, and nor had I sought it.

'You don't go out for dinner or –'

'We play games together. Sex games.' That was the whole point of the arrangement.

'So, there's no emotional involvement, no companion-ship?' He seemed saddened by the thought. 'I can't do that. If there's no emotion, no connection, then it's all down to plumbing and mechanics and what's the point in that? Isn't it just mutual masturbation?'

To be honest, I couldn't argue with that, but nor did I see the problem. When I'd first begun seeing the guys, I hadn't wanted that sort of closeness, or attachment. I was still bruised from my relationship with Craig. My freedom, the ability to act on my desires without recompense, had been more important to me than forming an intense emotional bond. It still mattered now, though I was less averse to letting someone in.

'We should go out to dinner,' he announced, like he was proving a point by taking me to a restaurant. 'Then we can get to know one another properly.'

If one of my other guys had said that, I'd have known he was looking for a route into my knickers, but Victor seemed more interested in getting into my head than my pants. I hoped he wasn't going to be too sadly disappointed by what he found there. I had to admit though, going out for dinner did sound nice. It'd be novel to sit and eat something and to not have the expectation of sex looming over me. If it happened, fine. And if it didn't ... then maybe that was fine too. Except that I did really rather want the sexy stuff to happen. Sod waiting, I wanted Victor now. I wanted my sticky fingers all over his body, and that meant getting on with what we'd allegedly come here to do. If he wanted to talk afterwards, then I wouldn't say no to a good old-fashioned cuddle while we kissed and told. I saw precious few of those.

'Should I take my jacket off?'

The question prompted a grin. He shook his head slightly, causing strands of black hair to fall over his face. 'If you like.'

I had only a vest top underneath, the fabric of which was thin and hugged my figure. It left little to the imagination, especially when, like now, my nipples were standing proud. 'What about the top?'

A smile tweaked his beautiful lips, and extended into his eyes, where it lit the hearts of his inky pupils. 'Keep everything on.'

'Everything?'

'Yes.'

Perhaps he'd changed his mind and didn't want me after all.

'Just undo your belt.'

OK. Now we were moving into territory I understood. I did so without prevaricating and waited for my next instruction.

'Are you aroused, Lyssa?' he asked, as he tapped out a rhythm against the worktop. 'What is it that's turned you on? Is it me? Or, are you excited because I might ask you to expose yourself?'

I touched my tongue to my teeth and bowed my head just a fraction, though I kept my gaze locked upon him.

He stopped drumming and curled his fingers around the edge of one of his work tables. His grip was so tight the effort was whitening his knuckles. He sounded calm, but I reckoned his heart was doing a drum roll not dissimilar to mine.

'If you were alone, how would you do this? Do you touch your nipples first, or is it straight to the prize?'

I brushed both palms downwards over my breasts. My nipples were sensitive, but I was impatient. Yes, sometimes, if my arousal was diffuse or marginal, I'd spend time pinching and twisting those peaks until they were red-flushed and ridiculously proud, but at present I was seeking swift gratification. I didn't think I could stand a prolonged tease. Therefore, I smoothed my hands downward towards my fly.

'No,' he barked, stopping me from pushing my hand inside. 'Not yet. Use the seam to ...'

'Uh-huh. Oh, God!' Yes. I understood. I didn't even need to really move my hand. I just had to press right over the ridge where all the leg seams joined and rotate my hips a little and ... and ... magic.

'How does it feel?'

'Not as good as if you were doing it.'

'Yeah – what would be different if I were doing it? You can't imagine I'd know how to touch you better than you know how to yourself.'

Maybe not, but I didn't have a crush on my own

80

fingertips. I wasn't anticipating the feel of them thrusting up inside my sex. Even if he let me wriggle them inside my knickers, they still wouldn't feel remotely as good as his nice hard cock. Not that I was altogether sure he was hard. The odd bubble zone lighting made it difficult to tell, especially as he was standing well back, almost as though he expected me to spring up at any second and cop a good feel of him. The notion was tempting, I admit it. If I actually pinned him in place and kissed him, I wasn't sure, but I didn't think he'd push me away.

It would be swift, but it'd be the end of things too. It would be betraying his trust. He'd asked me to keep my hands off, and until he gave me permission to do otherwise, that's what I was going to attempt to do.

However, that didn't prevent me from asking how he felt. He hadn't vetoed dirty talk.

'Are you hard, Victor?' His mouth puckered and his jaw seemed suddenly tight. I didn't back down. 'What do you think about when you're looking at me doing this?'

He remained quiet. His chest rose and fell a tad unsteadily. I figured he was aroused, just being stoic about it.

Although Victor possessed eyes like chips of hardened ice, they betrayed his emotions. They thawed, just like the winter frost leaving behind glittering glimpses of what lay within.

'Do you imagine these are your fingers, or that your

head is down between my thighs, licking me here? Can you taste me in your mouth? How do I taste? Do I make you want to go over the edge? What sort of dirty things do you want to do to me?'

He drew in a long breath through his nose.

'Shall I tell you what I want you to do to me?'

'Tell me,' he whispered, his voice so low, I barely heard him.

'I want to get down on the floor in front of you. Take you in my mouth and suck you. I want there to be two of me, so I can bend you over at the same time and tease you with my middle finger.' I lifted said digit to show him. I think he was clear on where I was suggesting I'd like to put it. 'Do you think you'd like that, Victor? Do you ever explore back there?' I felt sure he did. 'I want to bring you right to the edge, then stop and lick you all over. I want you to be mad with need when you finally get inside of me.'

'You know that can't happen.'

'I know "can't" isn't in my vocabulary. I'm not going to force you if the answer is no, but I hope that might change, and at some point you'll want me enough for the answer to be yes.'

'Why are you so sure I don't want you now?'

'Because you're over there and I'm over here.'

He gave a quiet hmpf. 'That's why I'm over here. I can't have you.'

He kept saying that. Can't … can't … can't. Naturally, I wondered why. We'd – at least I hoped – established that there were no impediments on my part, but what about him? What did I actually know about him? He'd already told me he wasn't married. What other sort of impediment was there? 'Are you … contagious?' It was an uncomfortable thought, and awkward to ask, but I had to, if only to rule it out. And it would certainly have explained his stand-offishness.

'No. I have a clean bill of health. There's nothing particularly weird about me that's not on public record.'

'Mm,' I replied, wondering if his voyeurism fetish was listed in his biography along with his pottery prizes. 'Then I'll take that "can't" as a "could, but I'm not willing to yet".'

'I guess.'

Oh, he was cruel standing there, all languid and nonchalant while my need bloomed so that the provocative rub of the seam against my pussy was no longer enough, and I needed something firmer and more direct.

'I need to undo my zip now, Victor.'

'How desperately?'

'Desperately.' Even without his permission, my hand had strayed to my zip, and the teeth were now sliding apart.

'OK, but turn around, kneel up on the chair, face the back. Don't let me see you, not properly.'

I could picture myself as Victor could surely see me. I was knelt with my knees apart, one arm supporting me against the back of the chair while the other rubbed with ever increasing urgency between my thighs. Only the curves of my bottom were exposed to him, the flesh creamy and smooth. Perhaps, he could see a shadow at the apex of my thighs. He could certainly hear my moans. I was finding it impossible to keep quiet. My clit had grown hard as a pebble and stood as erect as Victor's cock. I swear I heard slick sounds that weren't caused by my fingers, or the heel of my hand pressing against my clit. If he was – as I suspected – touching himself, I needed to see that.

'Don't. Turn. Around.'

No fair. I wanted to cry. He was touching himself. That soft swish was an absolute giveaway. He'd undone his fly and was massaging his shaft, up and down, matching my pace. Wasn't it enough that he'd already deprived me of one sense, must it now be two? 'Victor, I want to see you.'

'No.' The command was both sharp and firm.

'Then tell me what you look like. Describe what you're doing?'

'I think you know well enough already.'

'If it were me, I'd be stroking you from base to tip. I'd be rubbing the head against my lips, and tasting each bead of cum you're leaking as it issues from the slit.

Do you like to be sucked, Victor? Do you like it when a woman takes you in her mouth? I want to do that. I want to do it so very badly. Can't you let me? Not even a little taste?'

He made a sound, half choked, but wholly delicious. I was getting to him. He was rubbing and rubbing, unable to stop, but then, so was I. I was sailing into the sun, chasing something that rested on the very edge of the horizon. Almost there, I sighed and sobbed. 'Please,' I begged. 'Please just touch me. It needn't be with your cock, just give me your fingers to suck. Let me taste you.'

Of course, he didn't. He stayed in his corner and I in mine. I swore at him, called him impossible and unbearable, but that was only because I wanted him so very much.

'Don't speak,' he said. 'Just pretend I'm not here.'

As if that were remotely possible. 'You are here. You are. And I'm coming because of you.'

'Are you coming, Lyssa?'

Oh, God! Yes, I was. A hard tremor rolled through my tensed body. For a moment, I was rigidly stiff, my muscles all locked tight. Then with one beautiful sigh, everything relaxed. Pleasure rolled through me as a hot wave. I came, and I wept, and my orgasm still rolled on. Even when it was done and I was wiped out, and floppy and boneless against the chair back, there still remained a bright spark of something beating down below. It burned a little brighter as I heard him take one pace then a second, until I knew that if I turned, I'd find him standing right behind me.

'Damn, you're so beautiful. I know I shouldn't, but I've got to.' I didn't think he was really talking to me, more that he was articulating the thoughts running through his head. 'I just … I just really need to come.'

He did, right then and there. His sighs seemed to lock in place halfway up his throat, only to shoot out a moment later. The first splash of his cum landed right across the curve of my bottom. And my orgasm, which should have been done, reprised for one last incredible pulse.

'Ah, shit!' he said afterwards. His fingers hovered above my rear and the gift he'd given me. I think part of him wanted to rub it into my skin, but the larger part wouldn't let him. Whatever his reason was for insisting that we refrained from physical contact was at the forefront of his mind again. 'I shouldn't have done that.'

I turned around, but Victor already had his back to me. At least he didn't apologise. We both knew I wasn't displeased by how things had turned out. Indeed, I was already plotting how to push him further next time, so that his loss of control involved him getting all over me and inside me.

'Do you have some tissues?'

'God – yes, of course.' He passed a huge handful, then went to stand in the kitchenette while I cleaned up and straightened out my clothes. I went to him once I was presentable. We both stood beside the sink, Victor staring blankly at the window, me looking up at him. I liked that my sleek, black panther was somewhat ruffled around the edges. His clothing wasn't precisely square, there remained a pink flush of colour along the ridge of his cheeks, and his hair was in need of a comb.

I reached up to smooth the dark waves, only for him to turn and face me. 'I think I'd better take you home now.'

'And are you planning on coming in, once we get there?'

I didn't like the grim set of his jaw. 'It's already late.'

'Yes it is, but maybe we should talk.'

He tapped the very tip of my nose. 'We don't need to talk. We know where we stand. Going over it again won't change anything.

'OK. When are we going to see each other next?'

'Soon. Tomorrow if you like.'

I did like. I liked the idea very much and told him so. 'What shall we do – dinner?'

Victor shook his head. He collected our jackets and waited while I fastened my boot laces. 'Let's save that for mid-week. Maybe we could just visit a park or see a movie or something.'

'The cinema will be full of kids.' So would the park for that matter. 'Maybe we could just hang out together at my place.'

'Let's meet for a coffee in town, and we can take it from there.'

*Madelynne Ellis*

Diary Entry: Saturday 24 July (3 a.m.)

I can't decide if Victor's kinky or just
repressed. He seems determined to make things
difficult, even uncomfortable for us, when, if
he'd just relax his guard, or his morals, or
whatever it is that's stopping him, things could
be completely straightforward. Take just now
for example – I was so ready for him. All he
had to do was cleave his body to mine, and
I'd have been his. He'd have filled me up
exactly right. Not that I'm criticising what did
happen. I only wish I could replay it, so that I
could turn around and get a good look at
what he was doing. I want to watch him in
the same way he's watched me.

He wouldn't come into the house.

He wouldn't let me kiss him goodbye.

I dearly want to taste his mouth.

Tomorrow. I'm going to.

Why is he so afraid? Does he have body hang
ups? A hideous scar he's afraid to let me see?
Nothing about him could possibly repulse me. I
know if I manage to sleep now – I'm het up and
still turned on – I'm going to dream of him
coming all over me.

Diary Entry: Sunday 25 July

We met for coffee!

What's interesting is that Victor doesn't balk over touching me in a non-sexual way. It's only when there's a hint of deeper meaning, the flare of attraction between us, that he backs way and throws up that wall of reserve. Unfortunately, the more he retreats the more eagerly I want to tear down the barriers between us. I wish he'd tell me what that 'can't' really means, and what the criteria are for it becoming 'can'.

I'd like to know too, what it is that he finds so fascinating about me. Is it because I'm not afraid and that I'm prepared to expose myself or go after what I want sexually? And why does he find it so peculiarly intriguing that I'm certain I'll never settle down to another one guy, one girl relationship?

Maybe that's what his hang up is about. He already has a lover squirrelled away somewhere. Some other woman, who probably wouldn't approve of me, and he's biding his time to convince us both to share him and have sex with each other.

I guess I need to tell him I'm not in to other women. Now, if he wants me to share him with another man, that's a different story.

Except I guess he already knows this. Three of them to be precise.

PS: I still haven't heard anything from Nathan following his strop. It's not like him to throw his toys out of the pram in such a dramatic fashion, but I guess I'd be pissed off too if I thought someone had usurped my position. I was expecting a phone call from him first thing. I guess the fact that he hasn't called means he's still annoyed. That's fine, because I'm a bit cross at him too for yelling at Victor and making such a scene. Although Victor swears he's cool with everything, I can't help thinking that Nathan's attitude is part of what's holding him back from touching me.

Nathan isn't my boyfriend, though. He doesn't have a veto on who I date, or who I sleep with.

Damn, I want Victor so bloody much!

# Chapter Six

Victor?

I could hardly believe it when I saw him standing on the stairs at work. He was right on the turn, where the staircase splits in half, one way heading to the theatre restaurant and the other to the bar. How the devil had he slipped past me without me noticing? He seemed equally surprised to see me sat in my little cubbyhole of an office surrounded by promo postcards and theatre guides. I guess he'd dropped by and hadn't expected to find me so easily.

I leaned right over the desk and beckoned him over.

Victor hesitated. He looked around, and then suddenly those long thin legs of his stretched and he came ambling towards me, a smile creeping into his eyes and tilting up the corner of his mouth. It was like he'd always been looking for me, and now out of the blue he'd found me in this strange out of the way place.

I wondered if Sam had passed on the information

about my workplace along with my phone number, or if I'd mentioned it during one of the rambling talks we'd shared over the weekend. Just because I couldn't specifically remember it, did mean I hadn't let it slip. Not that it mattered, because he was here, in my place of work, and I was all of a tingle.

Work was part of my other life. Where I was ordinary, and had a boyfriend called Nathan, whom people supposed I'd shack up with one day. Victor would set tongues wagging, and necessitate some script editing on my 'normal life'. Still, I liked that he was here. I was ridiculously excited by it.

Victor came and stood right before the desk, blocking out the image of Leif Haralsson that Hattie was so enamoured of. Leif was cute, but Victor was sultry and sexy in an altogether more sinewy way. He'd dressed in a leather motorcycle jacket, with dark trousers that flared over the top of a pair of polished Chelsea boots.

'I'm due a break,' I explained, breathless with excitement. The foyer was empty apart from us. 'We can go somewhere just as soon as Stefan comes back.'

'Go where?' Victor asked, apparently unprepared for such a response. One neatly curved eyebrow tilted up his brow.

I'd only meant for us to grab a drink together, or maybe take a stroll outside, but then other, dirtier options filled my mind. Where in the theatre could we go, that was quiet?

'Actually, Lyssa, I can't stay for long. I'm on my way somewhere.'

'My break is only for a few minutes too.' I exited the booth, and joined him by the front of the desk. Stefan had just come through the staff door from the main offices and was headed our way. I signalled to him that I was taking five, and then hustled Victor towards Stage Door 3, which sometimes doubled as a conference room. The area was deserted today. It rarely saw any action except when a performance was taking place. Still, so as not to take any chances, I had a secondary barrier in mind, namely, the shuttered ice-cream kiosk that occupied one corner of the room and only opened at half-time during evening performances. 'In here,' I guided Victor.

He paused to look over his shoulder before stepping in. 'What are you up to, Lyssa?'

I shut the door behind us, and left the lights off. It made the inside of the kiosk gloomy, but there was enough light coming through the shutter slats to see by, and to allow us tiny glimpses into the room beyond. I knew the reverse wasn't true.

'This seems a bit extreme for a private conversation. I feel as though I'm in a spy movie,' Victor chuckled. He rested his back against the serving hatch.

Conversation didn't warrant such seclusion, but what I had in mind certainly did. We'd talked so much over the weekend that I didn't want to talk any more. I wanted action. I was an action kind of girl. 'Since you won't allow anything as normal as a quick kiss, I have to get inventive over letting you know how pleased I am to see you.'

He put on a serious face. 'Oh. And how pleased is that? Aren't you a little bored of me, considering how much you've seen of me this weekend?'

I didn't think I'd ever get tired of him. In fact, I was desperate to see a whole lot more. 'I'll show you how pleased, if you'll do the same in return.'

Victor's eyes narrowed slightly. 'Show me what?' His shoulders hunched too, betraying his wariness.

'A nipple,' I suggested, already seeking the buttons on my prim blouse.

Victor steepled his fingers, then curled them down so his hands were tightly clasped before his mouth. 'One nipple? I'm not sure how that's going to tell me how pleased you are to see me.'

I unbuttoned my blouse down to just below my breast-bone, and then pulled one side of the fabric down along with my bra. My breast popped right out of the lacy cup, the nipple beautifully pert. I thought it demonstrated my point perfectly. It certainly captured Victor's attention. 'Now you have to show me yours.'

His smile faded. 'Mine aren't nearly so interesting.'

'To me they are.'

He stared at the shutters a moment.

'I promise you, no one can see in.'

He wouldn't look at me as he unzipped his jacket, beneath which he wore a plain black T-shirt. I felt giddy as he clutched the hem, and then lifted it, until he was showing not one but both nipples, and a good deal more flesh besides.

I'd spent long hours wondering about what delights he was hiding under his clothes. Reality didn't disappoint. He wasn't built like Nathan, with slabs of corded muscle. He was, however, pleasantly defined, with thatches of dark hair across his chest and stomach. The latter thickened tantalisingly around the level of his trouser top. His actual nipples were two tiny brown pinpricks, not even the size of a penny.

'Satisfied?' he enquired. I could see he was itching to drop his clothing back into place.

'Of course not.' In order to be satisfied, I'd have had to spend hours, days even, exploring his body and getting to know every dip and hummock as well as all his sweet spots. Even then, I'm not sure I'd have had my fill.

'So ...'

Originally, I had some vague notion of getting him to strip one piece of clothing at a time, but we simply hadn't time for that and I strongly suspected that Victor would refuse. I was still surprised he'd consented to reveal as much as he had.

'So ...' I opened the ice-cream freezer that was

rumbling away behind me, and took out a large chip of ice. I tested it against my own nipple, and then passed it to Victor. 'Circle,' I instructed him.

'I'm not touching you, Lyssa.'

'I'm not asking you to.' In fact, I tucked my breast back into my bra. I wasn't even suggesting that it would be the ice in contact with me and not him. 'Use it on yourself.'

'Oh, no. It's cold.'

Of course it was cold that was the whole point. 'You keep leaving me with the chills. I think you need to know what it feels like to be left suffering.'

Our gazes locked. For a moment, I thought he'd refuse again, but instead, Victor touched the ice to one nipple. It immediately tightened.

'More,' I insisted. I reacted to his slow circles as if it were my nipples he was rubbing, except my nipples grew more pronounced, while Victor's seem to shrink and pucker from the touch. 'Rub it all over,' I encouraged. 'Now take it on a journey down. That's it. Slowly now. Slowly.'

Miraculously, Victor did as I instructed. I think once initial cold shock had worn off, he was more amused than aroused by the sensation. Leastways, he smiled a lot. I didn't mind if he thought it funny. Perhaps humour would serve me better, and if I made a joke of it, he'd allow me more liberties than if I'd simply demanded he take his clothes off.

'Lower. Lower.' As his hand circled across his abs and then his stomach, I imagined I was the one stroking him. 'Lower.' He hit the top of his fly, and stopped there, so that the cloth grew damp.

'I'm not seeing any ice trails on your skin, or your fly open.'

I nodded towards the freezer. 'You're more than welcome to assist me with either.'

Victor tilted his head slightly, a pose with which I was now becoming familiar. It said, I know what you're up to, and I'm considering my options.

'Besides,' I reminded him. 'You've seen it all before, whereas I haven't. Come on, Victor, give me a teeny peep.'

'There won't be anything worth seeing if this is involved.' He held the now shrunken piece of ice aloft, and it pinged from between his fingers and shot across the room, causing us both to raise our hands and then giggle as we failed to catch it.

Somehow in the brief commotion we ended up touching. For a split second, my palm brushed across his bare chest, and Victor touched my bum.

'Sorry. I'm so sorry.'

Despite the ice that had so recently chilled his skin, Victor burned with a ferocious heat. 'It's OK.'

I let that fact sink in a little before I decided to push for a little more. Maybe barriers were starting to crumble between us, and I'd get what I really wanted – his hot, hard body mashed against mine – a fraction sooner than I anticipated. 'Give me one little glimpse,' I begged him. 'I promise; no hands.' I even clamped them behind my back to prove my willingness.

'Haven't you seen plenty, already? Mine's hardly unique.'

In my experience cocks were as individual as the men they belonged to. I might have seen a few in my time, but Victor's was the only one I was interested in at this moment. Boy, was he being a tease. His long, agile fingers flicked back and forth over his trouser fastening as if he was actually debating whether to oblige me. I dared not hope he would actually do so.

'Victor.' I clenched my fists to prevent myself from ripping open his fly.

Yes, I wanted him that much.

'It's going to be quick, because I'm not standing around with everything hanging out,' he warned. The teeth of his zip started to part.

Victor wore plain black slips underneath. They covered less than a pair of skimpy swimming trunks, and certainly couldn't contain his current excitement. He only pulled the fabric aside for about a second. It was long enough to display his arousal. And long enough for me to know that his cock was just as slender and long as the rest of him.

'Beautiful,' I remarked, making him blush slightly. 'One more slightly longer look?'

I don't think Victor really enjoyed being admired. I guess it made him feel too self-conscious. I on the other hand enjoyed every second of seeing him. The second time, he pulled his things down so I could get a proper look. He was stiff and eager, and could have slid into me so easily. But I kept my word, even though my palms itched due to my desire to touch him. I thought of falling to my knees and using my mouth instead. That would only have been bending the rules, not breaking them, but I didn't do so, and perhaps that was just as well, since the stage door opened and a stream of people filed in from the auditorium.

Neither of us moved, though it was as if Victor suddenly snapped to attention: back, erection, the whole of him.

The crowd consisted of the actors from the current show, and I recalled they were doing some kind of workshop with a local theatre group today. One or two of them, Leif Haralsson among them, passed painfully close to the kiosk.

Victor held his breath.

They were just passing through, thank God.

The moment they were gone, Victor burst into motion. He was respectably dressed and out of the kiosk before I'd properly finished sighing in relief. 'I'll catch you later,' he muttered. Then he was gone.

Diary Entry: Monday 26 July

Sam phoned. She and David are worried about me. No need to guess what about. She even had the audacity to ask me if I was cheating on Nathan. Cheating! Since we don't have that sort of relationship to start with, how could I be cheating? For Christ's sake, considering how many times she's watched me with her husband you'd have thought she'd have realised that; but apparently, that was OK because Nathan was present!

Given that I refused to respond, she's no doubt reported back that I'm bonking Victor at every available opportunity. Sadly, not true. Although, I'm hoping today signifies we're a step closer to that.

As for Nathan, couldn't he phone me himself if he's concerned? Are we not adults?

Oh, hang on. He's not my boyfriend; he's just my fuck buddy, so he doesn't get to dictate who I see.

I'm almost tempted to phone Anthony tonight to ask him if he and Aaron would like to come over without any of the others. See what Nathan makes of that. I'll let Victor know of course, just in case he wants to watch.

*Confessions of A Greedy Girl*

Diary Entry: Tuesday 27 July

I came home from work last night horny as hell after spending most of the afternoon daydreaming about having Victor over every piece of equipment in the theatre box office.

He is going to give in eventually, isn't he?

I will go insane otherwise.

I haven't even had Hattie around to confide in/ pump for advice, as she's been on different shifts to me all week. Not that I'm sure she'll have the answer to: 'Help! What should I do? The guy I fancy the socks off only wants to watch me mastur- bate, and my other lovers are behaving like jealous asses.' It may be a bit outside of her usual field.

Didn't phone Anthony in the end, having decided it wasn't fair to use him like that. It was purely an excuse to call Victor and get him to come over. Of course, that meant I couldn't get to sleep. Too worked up. After spending an hour tossing and turning, I gave in and pulled the wand out. Crashed out with it still buzzing in my hand, having replayed every moment of Victor watching me or listening to me that we've shared. Thus followed a truly ace dream about him. Instead of Victor watching me, I was watching him.

101

For some reason, I'd gone to his studio. He didn't hear me coming up the fire escape, so I caught him unaware. The sun was streaming through the low windows and the skylights so that he was a black silhouette against the bright blue sky when I entered. At first, I thought he was taking five minutes off to think over some new piece of art, but then, when I got closer, it was plain that wasn't the case.

His top half was bare and not only was his fly undone, but his trousers were riding super-low down on his hips so that I had a clear view of him as he encompassed himself from root to tip.

I think women have this idea that for men, masturbation is all about swift satisfaction, that there's no finesse to it, and certainly no real brain involvement. Victor's strokes weren't like that. They were a feather-light dance of fingertips and slow circling, almost as though he were tiptoeing around his own arousal, much as he seems to do whenever we're together. I know I was at the centre of that fantasy though, because he kept repeating my name over and over, so that it became one long moan as he climaxed.

I don't think I've ever been as entranced by a man in the way I am about Victor. I have a physical craving, not just for his body, but to hear his voice. I'm not sure my willpower would prove strong enough to simply stand and watch him touch himself if it were to happen in reality. That sort of arousal, his desperation would prove too much. I'd probably take him, whether he wanted taking or not.

PS: Still no word from Nathan, and we normally see one another on a Wednesday night. I wonder if I've been dumped. Given the nature of our relationship, is that even possible?

Never mind, lunch with Hattie tomorrow!

# Chapter Seven

'He's gay,' Hattie announced over lunchtime baguettes in the theatre restaurant. Black and white stills of Leif Haralsson and cast graced the walls. Hattie bowed her head towards the nearest. 'He has a long-term partner he's been with since college that he adores. I took your advice and chatted to him the other night.'

I knew it, I crowed inwardly, Hattie's words confirming my suspicion that Leif was already taken. Cute guys always had someone waiting in the wings. Although I'd have plumped for attached or gay, rather than both. Still, for Hattie's sake, I muttered a sympathetic 'damn,' around a mouthful of egg mayonnaise.

'No probs.'

For someone who'd failed to secure a date with her dream man, she seemed remarkably cheerful.

'Seriously, Hats, I'm sorry about that. I mean it's obviously great for him that he's happily settled, but I know you were sweet on him.'

'Pah,' she snorted. 'It always was an idle daydream. I never really believed I stood a chance. I wouldn't even have spoken to him if it wasn't for you.'

'Oh, shit! I'm sorry.'

'Lyssa!' Hattie slapped the table in amusement. 'I'm not blaming you for anything. He's a nice guy. I had a fab evening chatting to him and a couple of the guys from lighting last Friday, and they've dropped by the box office a few times since. Besides, it could never have been more than a quick fling between us. He moves around too much because of his acting, and you know how I feel about uprooting. I get traumatised going on holiday for a week.'

'True.' Hattie was the biggest home body I'd ever met. If it wasn't for work, she'd probably have never left her house.

'Are you seeing the flamenco troupe tonight?'

Momentarily gobsmacked, I stared at Hattie, wondering how on Earth she'd found out about my boys. I was pretty secretive about them, so I couldn't see how word had got out, unless Victor had started snitching. Not that I actually thought that.

'Lyssa?' Hattie prompted a minute or two later. 'I'll take that as a no, shall I? I guessed you were planning to go after all the enthusing you did on the subject of wiggling male butts.'

'Oh, you mean that flamenco troupe.'

'Is there another one?'

The theatre was hosting an authentic Spanish group that evening, and Hattie was right. I had intended to buy tickets. 'I left it too late. We sold out. Besides, I'm doing something else.' Victor had phoned as I'd gotten ready for work that morning and arranged the dinner date he'd promised me. I rather hoped that he had something special planned in place of dessert, preferably, which involved multiple senses. It had struck me earlier that there were only so many variations of watching someone bring themself off, and we'd already covered most of them. Hopefully, once we'd exhausted his fantasy, then we could get on to indulging mine.

'Another date,' Hattie sighed, having finished a delicate bite of tuna. 'I wish my love life was half so exciting. Nathan must be completely mad for you. If only I had someone half so besotted with me.'

Perhaps it was time I 'fessed up. 'Look Hattie,' I began. 'About Nathan and I. It's not actually that serious, you know. We're really more like close friends with –' I had intended to say benefits, only she cut me off.

'Nope, not hearing it.' She waggled one perfectly manicured nail in front of my face, forcing a retreat into the back of my chair. 'Don't you give me the "it's not serious" speech, that's supposed to make me feel better. It doesn't work. Especially since I've seen the two of you together. No one sneaks off for that many quickies with someone they're not mad about. And you'd be mad not to be mad

106

about him. He's a thoroughly hot dish. How long have you been together now – since April?'

'March.'

'March,' Hattie parroted as if an extra month further substantiated her claim that Nathan and I were predestined soul mates.

The problem with her believing that was that it made it impossible to confide in her about Victor. 'It's just that –'

'Not hearing it. Lah-lah-lah.' Hattie clamped her hands over her ears. 'Honestly, Lyssa, you belittling what you have doesn't make me feel better about being a sad lonely singleton if that's what you're thinking. Nothing short of a man is going to do that.'

'You can have Nathan,' I mumbled. OK, I gave up. What was the point in trying, if the person you were trying to tell didn't want to hear it? It was especially irritating though, given that I didn't even know if Nathan was speaking to me at the moment.

'Tell me more about your meeting with Leif,' I prompted her.

'There's nothing more to tell. We just chatted. Besides, you can meet him in a minute. I mentioned we were having lunch today and he said he might join us.'

Perhaps it was just as well that I'd failed to enlighten her about my relationships. We'd never have been done before Leif arrived, and I didn't want my business shared among the actors.

'Look, he's here.' She pushed her chair back and rose. 'Leif, over here.'

I refused to turn my head and stare, instead choosing to focus on chewing my sandwich. He came up behind my chair, and circled the table to reach Hattie, who threw herself against his torso, so that her cheek pressed tight to his berry-coloured sweater. Her face nearly matched its colour. 'Can you stay long?'

Leif nodded agreeably. 'The school workshop group are still here for another hour, but they don't really need me.'

More than likely, he was pleased be rid of them. Teenage girls could be a handful at the best of times. I was surprised no ambulances had had to be called, given how disposed many of them were to hyperventilating when presented with anything exciting. And Leif Haralsson was exciting; even I could admit that.

I stole a few sly glimpses of him, while seeming to concentrate on my lunch. It was no surprise Hattie was besotted with his appearance. He really was a ridiculously good looking guy; tall and lean in that Scandinavian way, and possessed of beautiful bright-blue eyes. I saw a lot of actors, and in the flesh most didn't live up to their publicity shots. Leif Haralsson's publicity shots were some of the best I'd seen, but he remained striking, even devoid of make-up and studio lighting.

He smelled good too. Not in an overabundance of

expensive cologne way, but in a clean, fresh linen, subtly masculine way.

He turned around a chair from the empty table next to us and dropped his jacket over the back. 'Can I get either of you ladies anything?' he asked, digging his wallet out of his inside pocket.

'Oh, we're fine.' Hattie sounded breathless. She pushed the remains of her lunch aside. There was no question that Hattie was still smitten, despite her earlier remarks. Logically, she might have realised Leif was off limits, but no one seemed to have informed her heart of that fact.

Leif turned to me regardless.

'I've everything I need,' I replied, glancing up. Our gazes met.

'Oh, it's you,' he remarked as if we knew one another. His baby blue eyes widened a fraction, making him seem excited.

Of course, we didn't actually know one another. I can remember all my one-night stands, and Leif wasn't one of them. Yet he was staring at me as though he expected me to say something to confirm the connection.

'Sorry. I'm Lyssa.' I stood to shake his hand. His grip was a little too enthusiastic, so that by the time I was seated again, my cheeks were aflame too.

'You're friends?' Leif's gaze slid back to Hattie, before returning to me. 'I mean, yes, of course you are. You're both in the box office, right?' He gave a nervous laugh.

'That's right,' Hattie said.

'OK, then. Back in a moment.' He strode off towards the pastry counter.

'What was that about?'

I bowed my head to avoid meeting the particularly wounded look Hattie threw in my direction. I had no idea why Leif had acted so weirdly. 'I don't know. I swear it, Hattie. I've never even spoken to him before. Maybe he's got me mixed up with someone else. Look, I'm going to leave.' I stood, leaving my lunch half-eaten. Staying was only going to make things uncomfortable, and I wanted to make it clear to Hattie that I hadn't shagged Leif and wasn't trying to steal him away. 'You enjoy your chat. I need to shop for something to wear tonight anyway.'

'For your date with Nathan?'

'Yes,' I agreed, purely for expedience. If Hattie wanted to believe I was passionately involved with Nathan, then let her. Better that than her suspecting I was secretly bonking Leif. 'I'll see you Friday, OK.'

'See you, Lyssa.' She gave me a quick hug. 'Sorry I snarled.'

'Lyssa. Hi. You're looking very sexy tonight.' Nathan had his foot in my front door and was over the threshold before I had time to stop him, let alone explain that because he hadn't phoned to confirm anything, I'd arranged to go out with Victor.

110

'You're a rotten liar.' I was fresh out of the shower, still dressed in a bathrobe, and my hair hadn't seen a brush yet. Warily, I closed the front door. Considering our last meeting had ended with him stalking off, and the only communication we'd shared since had been via intermediaries, I wasn't sure what to expect. Had he come to chat, apologise or simply check up on me? My money was on the later. Someone had likely told him I was going out with Victor.

'Yeah, but babe,' he crooned, rounding on me the moment the latch clicked. 'You know I find near-nakedness sexy, especially when it's you.' He caught me around the waist, and somehow managed to pin me between him and the banister. 'What say I help you dry off a little, and then we can discuss what comes next. We did talk about doing cabaret tonight.' He ran his grip along my belt to where it was fastened at the front.

'Nathan, I'm going out with someone else.' I smacked his hand in order to dissuade him from picking open the knot. 'I don't have time to chat. I need to get dressed.' The dress I'd bought at lunchtime was hanging on the outside of my wardrobe, ready for me to slip into.

'Lys, it's Wednesday. That's our night.'

It was only our night by default. I shoved past him and headed for the stairs. 'Well, you didn't call, and we hadn't officially arranged anything. So, I made other plans.'

'With him, I suppose.' Nathan caught hold of me

again, this time from behind, and pulled me back against his body, so that his loins pressed tight to my bottom. His hot breath whispered against my ear. 'And where's he taking you?

I turned within his grasp. 'None of your business.'

Oh, but it was not what his expression said. He raised a hand and stroked my cheek in a way that made me jumpy. 'I was only asking. No need to get defensive. You know you could have rung and told me not to come over.'

Yes, well. He was making me nervous.

'How soon are you going? Maybe I could tag along.'

'No!' I blurted, barely able to comprehend anything more awful. I was looking for a nice night out; not an evening spent referring a snarling match. 'It's all pre-booked, and besides you're not dressed for it.'

'OK, then how about I head off when you do? You don't mind me hanging around for a chat while you get dressed, do you?'

He started up the stairs before I'd given him an answer, and somehow it was easier to roll with it than forcefully turn him out.

Nathan sat on the bed unobtrusively enough while I applied my make-up. He chatted about rugby fixtures and how much he'd bench-pressed at the gym last week. He even briefly veered onto politics and the current round of government reforms. It was the most normal discourse we'd ever shared, although it hardly qualified as a conversation, since I barely made a remark.

Having him present reminded me of living at home as a teenager, when getting ready for a date always seemed to involve an audience. My younger sisters would sit on the bed, playing dress-up with my prize lipstick, and would then howl and lie outrageously to Mum when I attempted to chase them off.

The trouble with Nathan started when I took the garter belt out. He stopped mid-gripe about the cost of fuel and stared.

'What?' I asked, although, perhaps it would have been better to ignore him.

'You're wearing stockings for him?'

Yes, that's right. I was. I proceeded to roll the first lace-topped nylon up my leg.

'Aren't you putting any knickers on?' He strained forward across the bed for a better look. 'My God, Lys, turn around, let me see.'

I remained side-on to the bed and concentrated on straightening out my hosiery. Stockings were fun. They did weird and wonderful things to men's brains, but they could also be a source of major stress when it came to getting the damn seams straight. However, I was gambling on the effort being worth it in order to win Victor over. Oh, I'd give him all the peeps he wanted – I could already imagine the light in his eyes when he saw the suspenders framing my sex – but I planned on ending tonight having had more than my own hands on me. It was time Victor stopped playing the tease and gave me a taste of something good.

The mattress groaned as Nathan rolled off the bed, and pushed up onto his feet. He came and stood too close, restricting my elbow room. 'Wow, he must be good if he warrants this sort of effort. What's he like, Lyssa? Have you even done it yet, or is this all because you're hoping to get lucky?' Nathan reached out, but stopped short of touching my bum.

I didn't bother to reply.

'Aw, come on. You don't need him to get lucky. You've got me.'

Had he always been this bigheaded? Why had that appealed to me?

'I've got exactly what you need, and I know the way you like it.' He circled his thumb over the top button of his fly.

'I happen to be looking forward to dinner.' I batted him out of the way, in order to put on my bra. The one I'd chosen for tonight was my all-time favourite. It produced the sort of cleavage that ought to have been outlawed. Also, unlike most of the underwear I owned, it wasn't black or white, but a deep burgundy that matched my suspender belt. Once upon a time, the set had also consisted of a teeny tiny thong, but that had disappeared moons ago and never reappeared. I actually suspected David of having stolen it. However, since none of my other underwear matched, yes, for artistic reasons I was going without.

OK, I admit, the notion of easy access hadn't entirely escaped me. I thought I had a handle on what Victor liked now too. It might take a herculean feat to convince him to shag me senseless in an alleyway or anywhere else, but it would surely take a lot less effort to entice him to put his fingers somewhere wet and warm in order to find out how desperately I needed to come. And of course, he could then persuade me to do something exceedingly naughty while he watched me.

Nathan's mouth continued to hang open as I shimmied into my new dress. The top half consisted of little more than two thin triangles that fastened behind my neck, and left most of my back on show. 'Good?' I questioned, twisting so the full skirt flared out giving him a glimpse of stocking tops. The fabric settled again, just above my knees.

'Babe.' He theatrically clenched one hand over his heart, while the other moved wistfully across his fly. 'You're wearing something over that, right?'

I'd thought about it, but he'd just convinced me not too. 'Nope. It's warm enough out.' And I'd only be outside for a matter of minutes between the taxi drop-off point and the restaurant door. If Victor had plans for us to go anywhere afterwards, then I was sure he could devise a way of keeping me warm.

I turned before the bedroom mirror, smiling secretively to myself. There was no doubt that the dress was an absolute winner. It looked better now than it had in the shop, which was a miracle in itself. Too often things I put on in store made me look and feel like a sack of potatoes at home. There were too many such examples occupying space in my wardrobe. This time round, I'd definitely bagged a bargain. Not only did the dress emphasise all my good bits, while disguising the less endearing ones. It had also been reduced, meaning I'd bagged a designer dress for a bargain price. Now all I had to do was go and bag myself Prince Charming too.

With that thought in mind, I bent over, giving a merry wiggle, in order to slip on my favourite strappy heels.

'Christ!' Nathan blurted, from behind me. 'You're going to stop the traffic. Are you doing this on purpose? For God's sake, don't bend down while you're out.'

He rushed over to help me stand, an offer I refused in favour of smoothing my skirt over my rear. I seriously doubted I'd shown anything off. Nathan was just determined to sidetrack me. 'Only if Victor asks,' I teased. It was worth it for the look on his face, a half-crazed mix of fury and lust.

'Damn it, Lyssa. Why are you doing this? Why are you dressing like this for him instead of me?'

'I'm not. I'm dressing like this for me.' The fact that I hoped the outfit also enticed Victor was entirely incidental.

'Look, what's this about?' he demanded. I think he'd liked to have shaken me. 'Aren't I good enough anymore? Do you need more of a challenge? More ... extreme stuff.' He stretched to find the right word, but to honest, I wasn't sure there were any right words. I liked Nathan. I enjoyed what we did together, but I'd never obsessed over him like I did over Victor. Love wasn't part of our relationship. We had sex. We had a good time. But there was nothing deeper gluing us together.

'I suppose you realise you're going to cripple him the moment he sees you.'

Not quite cripple him, I hoped.

'He's going to be too hard to walk. I doubt he'll even manage to stumble with you as far as the rest room.'

'To do what, Nathan. He's not interested in sleeping with me. He just wants to buy me dinner.'

That was a minor bending of the truth, but so what. It was worth it to see Nathan's reaction.

'The fuck he does. He's not meeting you in order to watch you slurp noodles. Not unless he's a real sicko. He's after sex, the same as any other man. OK, it might be screwed up voyeuristic sex, but it's still sex, and you know it.'

'So?' I shrugged. 'It's not as if I'm an inexperienced

virgin in need of protecting. I know what men want, Nathan, and I know what I want too. And I have to say I'm rather looking forward to it.'

Nathan slowly shook his head as if he couldn't quite credit what he was hearing. The motion caused his hair to fall over his eyes. Irritably, he shoved it back out of the way. 'You're being cruel, Lys. I swear you're only doing this to torture me. What did I do? Did I mess up somehow? If so, just tell me and I'll make it right again.'

OK, so maybe he was starting to make me feel slightly mean. I gently patted Nathan's hand. 'I like him, Nathan. He fascinates me. He's complex, and I haven't figured him out yet. Maybe he won't entice me so much once I do, but meanwhile …' I collected my purse.

'Hang on, Lys. Wait. At least be reasonable.'

'What?'

He walked his fingers over one curve of my bottom. 'Don't leave like this. Let's just make friends again.' He smoothed the same hand down the back of my thigh to the hem of my dress. Seconds later his fingers were warming the soft stretch of skin above my stocking top. 'I need you. Even if it's just for a minute or two; otherwise, I'm going to have the image of him all over you burned into my brain for the rest of the evening.'

'Oh, get off.' I rolled my eyes as I smacked his hand away. I wasn't even sure if he was genuinely upset or just trying his luck.

Nathan put his hand right back where it had been. 'Please, Lys. You've time if we're quick.' Bronze flecks shone in his deep, puppy dog eyes. 'Go on, be a sweetie.'

'No.' This was ridiculous. So ridiculous I couldn't help smiling at the absurdity of it. 'A) I'm not in the mood. B) I'm seeing someone else, and C) I absolutely don't have time, even if I was interested.' Which I wasn't. The bedside clock showed eight. I was due to meet Victor in thirty minutes, of which the taxi ride would take up ten.

'Aw, come on,' he coaxed, nuzzling closer. His hand kept on stroking, back and forth, sending pleasant, anticipatory tingles through my flesh. 'It'll put some colour in your cheeks.'

D) Nor did I plan on arriving smelling of Nathan.

'I have rouge for that.'

'I could take the edge off your need,' he wheedled. Quite what he envisaged me doing, I wasn't sure. Maybe he thought I'd be so overwrought with lust, I'd leap on Victor the moment I saw him and bonk him on the table in the middle of the restaurant.

'Let me just –' To my astonishment, Nathan dropped onto his knees, and then somehow his head was under the front of my dress, and that hand was no longer circling over my rear but stroking upward along the inside of my thigh. 'Wow, so wet.'

'Nathan.' It was too late. He already had me. Yes, I really was that weak-willed. The moment his mouth

119

met with the soft, plump folds of my slit, I was his. His tongue flicked out and sent electricity crackling through my synapses. Muscles and tendons pulled tight. It was as though I'd been jacked into the mains. I guess I hadn't realised just how worked up lusting after Victor for a week had left me. My body knew though, and it, unlike my head, didn't give a damn where the relief came from.

Nathan's mouth was so soft, and the flick of his tongue so sweet, that instead of resisting, when he said 'Open your legs' I obeyed. I stood in my towering heels, clinging to his head and let him lick me into submission.

Clearly, I'd been overlooking or underusing Nathan's talents, because boy did he know how to use his tongue. I was on cloud nine in minutes, muscles locked tight, just about keeping me upright as my orgasm built and then shook me.

If he'd been gentlemanly, and left it at that, then I could have slipped out of the door merry as a babe, secure in the knowledge that Nathan wasn't going to be a pain and that he'd still be around to give me a good seeing to if Victor failed to deliver, or it just didn't work out.

Alas, Nathan had no intention of allowing me to make this a one-sided arrangement. While I was still languid and floppy, he tipped me backwards onto the bed.

'Mm,' he hummed, as he lodged himself where I unfortunately have to admit I really did want to feel it. 'I really can't let him have all the fun, now can I? There now.

There.' I lifted my hips to greet him. 'Isn't that good? Isn't it right?'

It was something neither good nor right, but my body reacted all the same. It welcomed him. Clove to him. Maybe we did have just about enough time. If we were quick, I'd only be a minute or two late. Maybe I could even explain truthfully to Victor why I was late. Considering he hadn't objected to watching me with Nathan, perhaps he'd enjoy hearing about my adventures with him too.

Or maybe I was being a fool.

At that moment it didn't matter, because it felt so damn good to have Nathan inside of me.

'Babe.' Nathan pushed his hands beneath my bottom, and lifted me to meet his thrusts. The position made things tight, and dragged his cock over my clit every time he lifted. 'You're good, Lys,' he cooed. 'The best. That's so damn sweet.' He'd found the perfect angle for both of us. He sought my mouth and kissed in the same demented, demanding way that he was taking me. It left me breathless and lightheaded. Only one thing mattered any more – the ache between my thighs.

'Close,' he puffed. 'Tell me what you need. Are you going to come for me again?'

I absolutely was. Even if he stopped dead right at this moment, I'd still have gone off.

'Together,' he insisted. 'Together.'

When it came to matching orgasms, I'd never found timing was all that perfect. However, on this occasion, everything seemed to fall into place. I bucked, and Nathan bucked too. I soared. He gasped. When my climax finally broke, Nathan was with me.

Finally spent, he flopped down on top of me and smeared a sloppy kiss across my jaw. 'See, I told you we had time.'

It was plain wrong that he could make me feel so good, and then make me want to murder him. Nor was I overly impressed a moment later, when with a self-satisfied sigh, he proceeded to pull up his pants.

'Aren't you going to clean up?' I asked.

'Nah. I kind of like the fact that you're all over me. Now when I think of you out with that idiot, it won't matter so much because I'll know that I had you first.'

God – I'd been such an enormous fool! This hadn't been about any sort of bond between Nathan and I. He'd just been out to prove he was still the alpha male. Worse still, not only was I now late meeting Victor – goddamn it, had time sped up? – I'd just had unprotected sex with an imbecile. Sure, I'd taken my birth control pills, but I also made condoms an absolute rule and Nathan knew that. He didn't even have the grace to look contrite. In fact, he wore enough of a grin to make me suspect the omission had been completely deliberate, rather than heat of the moment forgetfulness.

'Why?' I demanded.

'Lys,' he laughed. 'It's no big deal. We're both clean. You're on the pill and I, at least, am not shagging anyone else. Besides, I rather like being shiny with you. We should do it more often.' He leaned forward and stole a kiss. My reaction was too slow to fend him off.

'Bastard! You wanker.' I hit him across the back as he pressed me down into the eiderdown.

'Now you're not mistaking me for your chum, Victor, are you? Stop this, Lys. Think on it. Your pussy certainly wasn't complaining about the attention it got. You were milking me like you'd never get enough. So quit snarling.'

'Get off me.' I thrashed around, but he wouldn't release his grip, nor did I have any real chance of breaking it. Nathan had more muscle in one of his biceps than I did in both arms.

'Tell me truly that you're not still hot for me, that you don't want any more, and I will.'

'I'm late to meet him now.'

'Forget about him. I'm talking about us.' He sought my gaze and held it. His big puppy dog eyes failed to cow me.

'Let go.'

He didn't, but he did shift positions so that he was sat astride my hips, rather than pressed along the whole length of me. 'Seriously, Lys, you need to decide what it is you want and who, for that matter. You've always been greedy, and until now I've been accommodating, but there has to be limits. So, decide – is it me or him you want? And don't imagine for a second that he'll be half so indulgent.'

'Is that an ultimatum?'

He sniffed. 'I'm just suggesting you think carefully before you choose him over me.'

'What the hell is the matter with you? You've never been like this over anybody else.'

'You're not like this over anybody else. I'm supposed to come first, Lys. That's always how it's been. You're the one who isn't playing by the rules anymore.'

'What rules?' There'd never been any rules. Unless the rules had been, let's fuck like crazy whenever any of us fancy it.

'Stay with me.' His voice dropped to a more even tone. 'Come on.' He kissed my neck, and the top of my breasts. 'I'll spend the night.'

Nathan had never spent the night with me, and I had no intention of making this our first sleepover. There were things he could have offered me that might have made me stay. Things like that long desired threesome, but Nathan wasn't actually interested in pleasing me, all he wanted was to stop me from seeing Victor.

'Let go of me, Nathan.'

'You don't mean that.'

'Yes, I do.'

Reluctantly, he released his hold, allowing me to wriggle my way out from beneath him. I sat up, rubbing my wrists. 'I think you'd better leave now.'

His expressive eyes darkened, and became angry. He looked at me as if I were dirt, less than dirt, something he would turn his nose up at even touching. 'Lyssa, if you send me away now, you will regret it.'

Considering how high the price of his attention suddenly was, I didn't think so. 'Go. Really, Nathan, just go.'

He rose off the bed, shaking his head. 'I can't believe you're being as selfish and shallow as this. You're making a big mistake, Lys, throwing everything away, everything we've built, in pursuit of a daydream. What do you even know about the guy? Nothing,' he answered for me. 'How do you know he's going to give you what you want?'

I didn't. That was part of the fun. What I did know was that I liked Victor. I also appreciated the fact that he didn't try to manipulate me, something Nathan did rather too well.

'Well, don't expect me to sit around waiting for you to see sense, and don't expect the others to do so either.'

That sounded rather like a threat, something his set jaw and hunched shoulders also seemed to project.

'Leave. Right now. And don't call.'

'Honey,' he drawled layering sarcasm into his tone, 'I wasn't going to.'

It was only once the front door slammed did the finality of what had happened sink in. Nathan had effectively put an end to us, or I had. It was unclear to me which of us had struck the death blow. The view in the bedroom mirror was no longer a pleasant one. I was a mess; or rather I looked exactly like a woman who'd been fucked, both figuratively and literally. My make-up was smeared; there were marks on my breasts and neck. Hell, there were even bruises on my thighs. Tears of frustration welled as I hobbled back into the bathroom. They fell thick and fast as I re-showered. Would the others, as Nathan predicted, abandon me too? None of them had thrown hissy fits. They weren't part of a hive mind, but they were first and foremost Nathan's mates.

Who would make me feel special if they were gone?

Did I even dare hope the answer might be Victor?

# Chapter Eight

'I'm afraid that Mr Alexander left a few minutes ago.'

Despite the maître d's insistence, I took a moment to scan the sea of cosy tables for signs of Victor. There were few single occupants amongst the diners, and none bore any resemblance to him. Even from behind, I'd have known him immediately. I was sure after our last time together that I'd committed every detail of him to memory. He was my focus now, which was why I was having so much trouble accepting he'd gone. 'You're sure?'

'Quite certain, miss, I called the taxi. He left fifteen … twenty minutes ago.'

He'd waited over an hour. I could hardly blame him for heading home at that point. He must have thought I'd stood him up, especially as he'd tried to reach me by phone too and I hadn't replied. His initial calls had gone unheard while I showered; I'd only picked up the missed call notifications in the taxi. His last attempt had been a text message. He'd politely enquired:

Where are you?

If our situations had been reversed, I knew my message would more likely have read, 'F. U.' I guess that showed which of us was the more patient and kindly.

'Can you tell me where he headed? Did he go home?'

The waiter continued to frown over his pepper grinder. The queue of other patrons had grown while I demanded answers, and now snaked out of the door. 'I couldn't possibly say. Perhaps if you contacted him to find out.' He stared pointedly at the phone clutched within my hand.

I wasn't completely stupid. I'd already tried to reach him that way, but his mobile was switched off, and I kept being put through to an annoyingly nasal lady, who told me how much a voicemail message would cost. The waiter shrugged. I suppose it really wasn't his problem. I left the restaurant faced with two choices; to go home to an empty house, or I could attempt to track Victor down. Since I didn't have a residential address for him, my only option was to try his studio.

The night air bit into my shoulders as I scuttled back along the pavement, to where, miraculously, the private hire car I'd arrived in was still idling by the kerb. I knocked on the window.

'I can't take you, love.' The driver pointed at the unlawful hire sign on the passenger-side door. 'You'll have to call the office, or head along to the taxi rank at the end of High Row.'

'Yes, but I did call and book you,' I insisted, giving him my best smile, as I climbed into the rear. 'This is the wrong place. I need to go somewhere else.'

'Right,' he grumbled, squinting back at me as though he suspected me of some deep moral wrongdoing. I guessed my party frock didn't meet with his approval, or rather it did, but he'd never let his daughter out wearing so little. 'Where to, then?'

I rattled off the name of the industrial estate, which prompted a deeper squint.

'I'm meeting someone. He's working late.'

'As you say.'

By now I suspected he had me pegged as a call girl. Rather than disabuse him of the notion, I ignored him in favour of checking my phone again. I had a four bar signal, but no new messages, despite having sent Victor a dozen. When I phoned, the call went straight through to the annoying lady again.

Ten minutes later, I paid for the ride and waited for the car to leave before heading for the spindly fire escape that led up to Victor's studio. A faint light shone out of the windows above. It seemed my instincts had served me well. All I had to do now was hope he'd accept my apology.

The iron stairs were no less treacherous second time

around. After stumbling only two steps into the ascent, I stripped off my stiletto heels, and patted upwards wincing at the pain of the cold metal against my stocking-clad feet. The faint strains of music whispered from above, something melodic from the dawn of pop that I couldn't put a name to. Flickering orange light bled across the topmost rungs of the fire escape. The studio door stood partially ajar. I almost expected to peep within and find Victor at his potter's wheel, perhaps bared to the waist having stripped away his veneer of civility – shirt, cravat, waistcoat and jacket – in order to pour his frustration into his art.

It was clear to me now that I ought to have dealt with Nathan properly when he'd first arrived, instead of passively letting him rule the roost. Still it was too late now. I couldn't undo the last few hours, only attempt to mend the damage.

I knocked, only to receive no answer, nor could I see anyone within from the doorway. After a second knock achieved identical results, I let myself in.

Since my last visit, Victor had erected a Z-shaped storage unit that bisected the long room, creating smaller zones. The area closest was brightly lit by several standing lamps, though the rear of the studio lay in near darkness. I dropped my shoes by one of the packaging crates and waded a little deeper. 'Victor? Are you in here?' Given the volume of the music now I was inside the building,

I doubted he could hear me. 'It's Lyssa. I'm really sorry that I was late.'

I approached the darker end of the studio, and nearly walked into a chair that lay overturned at my feet. I bent, meaning to set it to rights, only instead I caught a glimpse of bare leg through the hollows between the unit's shelves. 'Victor!' Alarm set my heart thumping. I scrambled past the chair and rounded the end of the unit, not to find Victor, fallen and hurt, but to come face to face with Leif Haralsson. Naked.

For a moment, I stood like a rabbit in the headlights. We'd have been staring at one another, if not for the fact that Leif's eyes were closed.

He wasn't alone. There was another man knelt before him. Hattie had told me Leif was happily settled. She'd even mentioned it was a gay relationship. Sadly, that didn't take the sting out of learning who his partner was.

Certain things made perfect sense now, like why Victor had been at the theatre that day. He'd been to see Leif, not me.

Victor had always denied that he was particularly voyeuristic. His actions had seemed to speak louder than words, but his reticence was abundantly obvious now.

He hadn't wanted to cheat. And stumbling across me doing naughty things wasn't remotely the same as actually doing the evil deed with me. One was pure chance, the other planned devilment.

131

I didn't approve, but it was logical. I couldn't help thinking that some honesty might have served him better. One thing I didn't understand was why he'd shown an interest in me in the first place. Who'd want to swap Leif for me warming their bed? And why the devil hadn't Victor told me he had a lover, considering he knew that I had several.

I knew many women would have about turned and left at this point, but I wasn't a typical girl. I didn't mind that Victor had another lover. I was only a little cross that he hadn't told me. Why hadn't he simply said 'Hey, Lyssa, you know, I really do fancy you, but I'm with Leif Haralsson at the moment. I'm not sure how to work it out, so while I figure it do you mind if we just hang out'. It would have sounded pretty crazy, but it would at least have been truthful, and miles more honest that his concocted aversion to touch.

The other reason I stayed was so Victor realised I hadn't stood him up. As right now wasn't a good point to announce that fact, I scuttled back behind the Z-shelf, determined to wait until they were finished before announcing myself.

The minutes passed exceedingly slowly perched on top of a packaging crate. I had nothing with which to pass the time and a head full of unanswered questions. Worse still, I could hear everything. The slick sounds a mouth makes when it slides along a man's length; the soft swish of fingers on skin, and skin moving against skin. I knew the moment things got intense; heard the soft inhalation of breath that preceded the gasp as one man welcomed the other. I'd longed to see two men make love, yet here I was eavesdropping on their passion but without the images to make it fully realised.

Who was on top? Who was on the bottom? Was their relationship that straightforward? Perhaps they switched around. Were they facing, or had Leif bent Victor over one of his many workbenches so he could take him from behind?

The longer I sat, the more desperately I needed to know.

I turned. There were numerous gaps between the books stacked on the shelves. If I bent a little, and rested just so, it was even comfortable to stand and peep through.

Victor was no longer on his knees. Instead, he sat perched on the edge of a workbench, with Leif pressed tight to his front. All I could really see was Leif's arse, and what a pert piece of perfection it was; firm and tight, with enough definition to make it truly scrumptious. It was the sort of arse – and really no other word would do – that was made to sport finger marks, just as his broad, lean back was perfect for scratches.

They were together, locked in a rhythm of tension and release, Leif's hips driving the pace. Their mouths moved with hungry familiarity, groans expressing what words couldn't. This was no chance encounter, not that I'd ever assumed it was. No, this was two men who knew one another inside out. There were no tentative touches. I saw no indecisiveness. Only sure strokes and building need.

I'd waited for this chance and now I was seeing it, it wasn't quite how I'd imagined the occasion to be. In all my fantasies my presence was acknowledged. I watched only until I was encouraged to join in. This on the other hand was spying.

That gave me a few guilty pangs, but they were swiftly eliminated. After all, I was only doing what Victor had done. It wasn't as if the first, or even the second time he'd watched me, he'd ascertained consent.

The heat Victor and Leif generated quickly warmed my cheeks. Other parts grew plump and moist. If the option of joining in had been presented, I'd have been naked so fast you wouldn't have seen me move. I wanted Victor, had done so since I first saw his reflection in the mirror at the gallery. Now, I longed to press myself to Leif's back, to follow the roll of his hips with mine, so that it would almost feel as though I were him – that I was the instrument of Victor's pleasure, and that my kisses and nips were leaving bright marks on his pale, pale skin.

How Victor maintained such restraint when he watched, I couldn't grasp, for as my arousal quickened, a simple wriggle that squeezed my thighs together wasn't enough. I had to touch myself, but even then the pinch of fingers against my nipple wasn't enough. I needed direct stimulation right between my thighs.

At least I'd dressed to make things easy.

A slick welcome greeted my questing digits, making the glide over my clit silky smooth. I gained no relief from it, only a maddening desire to rub harder and faster, to match my pace to the clench and release of Leif's beautiful arse.

'Yes. Oh God, yes,' he moaned, driving into Victor a little harder. I wished I could zoom in for a direct close-up of Leif slipping in and out of Victor.

'You don't deserve it, but fuck that's good.'

Why didn't Victor deserve this treat? Maybe it wasn't a treat, perhaps it was a punishment. That notion just kicked my lust-o-metre into meltdown mode. Was this display of rough male loving, a reaction to my involvement with Victor?

'You forgive me though.' I could see Victor, now their positions and mine had shifted a bit. Bookends pressed hard against my chest. Victor was all twinkly eyed and flushed. His mouth red, and bruised from countless kisses.

'Who says I do? Just because your arse is sweet doesn't mean I'm not pissed off with you.'

Victor pushed at Leif's shoulders, as if to create a few inches of distance between them. 'You've no reason to be. Nothing happened.'

They were definitely talking about me.

'No sly kisses,' Leif enquired.

If only there had been.

'None.'

'Then what have you been tempting her with – a few dirty words, maybe?'

Victor turned his head to avoid Leif's gaze. The blond man laughed and taking hold of Victor's hips rammed into him again and again, until they were both panting. Between my thighs was a sopping, streaming mess. My nerves were singing, and I was straining to hear every word they said.

'You know, maybe that's why she stood you up. She probably got a better offer from a man who was actually prepared to put his dick where he'd promised to shove it.'

That's not it. It wasn't the reason.

'She knew where the line lay, I made it perfectly clear. I don't know why you're being so sanctimonious about it anyway. I kept my distance so as not to hurt you.'

So Victor really had wanted me.

Leif's shoulders and head shook as a dry chuckle rumbled in his throat. 'You've some weird notions about distance. Next you'll be telling me it was entirely platonic. Oh, I believe you haven't kissed her.' He raised two fingers before Victor's lips to silence his reply. 'I even believe you haven't fucked her, but I bet there are plenty of dirty boundaries you have crossed. What have you done? Did you whisper sweet nothings? Have phone sex? Get off at opposite ends of the same room?'

'I … I didn't plan it.'

'What was wrong with doing things the way we've done them in the past? You could have come to me and said "Leif, I've met this girl that I find totally hot. How do you feel about me inviting her over one night for some raunchy fun?"'

They parted, but only for seconds as Leif wrestled Victor across the workbench, onto his stomach. He didn't test his readiness with his thumb, just pushed straight back into Victor's rear. 'I could have come out for dinner with you tonight and we could have taken it from there. At least then you wouldn't have been sat there alone when she didn't show, and I wouldn't have to be taking you like this to stop you slitting your own wrists.'

'I'm annoyed, not suicidal,' Victor retorted. I didn't catch all of what they said next. I was too busy digesting the fact that they'd previously shared women. Like it wasn't unusual to pick a girl up and bring her back to their bed. I wanted to shake Victor and ask him why he hadn't done as Leif suggested too.

'Am I supposed to believe that she's some timid little mouse that'd have kittens at the thought of being taken by two blokes at once? Because I know that's not the sort of woman you go for. You like them wilful and greedy.'

A less honest woman would have balked at that

137

description. I was happy to admit to being both, especially if it got me where I wanted to be. I almost, almost admitted my presence.

Victor was having trouble speaking. He was moaning with increased vigour, for gone was the earlier sense of affection that had defined Leif's touch, replaced by boiling anger. 'No – not saying that,' Victor managed to gasp around a string of involuntary groans. They were both lathered with sweat. Victor was definitely close to coming apart.

'Then why didn't you, eh?' I jumped as Leif's palm cracked across Victor's buns. He grabbed hold of Victor's shoulders and jerked him a fraction more upright. 'Why, Victor? 'Cause I'd love to know.'

'Yes,' I echoed, my fingers working furiously. I was so, so close now. 'Tell me.' I wanted to know too.

Victor's long, clever fingers curled tight around the table edge, helping him brace himself against Leif's thrust. He didn't speak for the longest time. I think he was hanging on the very edge of release.

'Come on, Victor, I want to hear it.' Leif dragged his lover upright, so they were sandwiched together, sadly facing away from me, though I could see their silvery outline in the dark of the windows. Leif's hands roved across his lover's chest and stomach, before moving downwards to clasp his shaft. 'You want to come now, don't you? Well that's the admission price.'

Victor croaked something. I didn't catch it and nor did Leif, whose hand worked frantically at Victor's erection, circling and circling over the exposed and sensitive head. Victor's lips were drawn back exposing his clenched teeth.

'You'd better say it again.' Leif prodded him relentlessly. The pad of his thumb pressed somewhere I knew to be exquisitely sensitive. Victor was teetering on a knife's edge and I was standing there with him ready to fall the moment he made his revelation.

'I want more than one night with her.'

I was falling ... falling and coming. Not for a minute had I anticipated that response. He hadn't claimed to love me, or muttered anything involving forever, but nonetheless the admission was a mighty step in that direction. It told me that I was wanted, and that he'd thought about it. It hinted at the formation of a special bond, something akin to what he already shared with Leif. Hence my orgasm pounded like a line of cannon fire ... boom ... boom ... boom as I clutched tight to the bookcase for support. Only a sheer miracle and the fact that my muscles had locked tight stopped me from actually toppling.

It was only in the moments afterwards, when the taste of iron hit my tongue that I realised I'd bit my lip so hard in an effort to keep quiet that it'd bled. It was then too, that I realised the men had broken apart. Victor lay prone against the tabletop; wrung out and sticky with his own cum.

Leif had crossed to the window. 'You'd better explain that,' he said, when Victor pushed himself tentatively upright. 'Because it sounds suspiciously like you're looking for ways to slip her into our relationship.'

'What would be so wrong with that? Wouldn't it be nice to share someone we care about, instead of it always being some faceless woman whose name I can't even remember the next day? Yes, I like Lyssa. Yes, she excites me. She's fun, Leif. And wicked too.'

Victor left the workbench and crossed to where his lover stood. 'That said, I hope you realise you'll always come first. You do know that?'

'No. Actually, I don't.' I hadn't imagined anyone as gorgeous as Leif could be quite so insecure. He slapped away Victor's outstretched hand, and fished around in the mound of discarded clothes until he found his trousers.

'Nothing's changed,' said Victor. He snaked his arms around his lover's torso, and refused to be shrugged off. 'And you know if you're adamantly against this, then we won't do it. I would have introduced her if things had gone right this evening.'

'And what if I'd disliked her? I have met her, you know. She works at the theatre, but I'm sure you already know that.'

'I wasn't about to force her on you.'

'Weren't you?'

'You're the most important thing in my life. I'd never sacrifice that.'

'Then perhaps we should both be glad she stood you up, because now we can forget about it.'

Leif sounded pleased about that. Victor looked saddened

'Yes,' he sighed. 'Perhaps it's best it's all over.'

With one little phrase I'd been dismissed. Flown was the possibility of ever finding myself in bed between them, or of even having Victor to myself. And though I could curse Victor for giving up on me, and Leif for being jubilant about it, I knew I only really had myself to blame. If I'd sent Nathan on his way an hour sooner, and met Victor at the time we'd arranged, then things might have worked out differently.

I didn't stay to announce myself. What was the point at this juncture? The important decisions had already been made. Leif wasn't willing, and Victor had already tidied me into a box marked 'past mistakes'.

Maybe they heard me pattering down the fire escape at full tilt. I don't know. I didn't look back to find out. Only once I'd left the little industrial park did I even slow my pace and notice that in my rush I'd left my shoes behind. In amongst Victor's clutter, they'd probably go unnoticed for weeks.

Once on the main road, I limped towards a bus shelter. Here the traffic purred as it rushed by, and the dark shop

windows glowed with the reflected colours of the street
lights and passing cars. I flopped down and called a cab.

Once home, I sent a final text to Victor.

Goodbye.

There wasn't anything else to be said.

Diary Entry: Wednesday 28 July

Christ, what a mess. I'm glad I'm off work
tomorrow. If rowing with Nathan and putting up
with his shit wasn't bad enough, now everything's
gone sour with Victor. I blame Leif for it, even
though I can sort of understand why he doesn't
want to share. I hope he doesn't come to the
ticket desk to speak to Hattie again. It's not as if
there's anywhere to hide, and what am I
supposed to say to him? 'Hi, Leif. Sorry I didn't
get to shag you and your lover's socks off. I bet it
would have been fun.'

Because it absolutely would have been fun. Too
bad he wasn't prepared to give it a try.

# *Chapter Nine*

The next morning I woke to the sound of persistent ringing. Clothed in a fluffy dressing gown, I stumbled down the stairs to yell at whoever was playing musical doorbells. If it turned out to be the postman with a parcel for next door I was going to give him such an earful. 'Yes,' I growled, as I yanked the front door open

'And good morning to you too, my lovely.' Anthony's smile threatened to engulf the rest of his features. The bright dawn sunlight filled his blond hair with golden streaks and formed a halo around his head. I suppose I'd been praying for a miracle, but Anthony was no angel of the Lord, come to set this sinner straight again. He was here to lay a carpet.

'Good night, was it? Does poor lickle Lyssa have a sore head?' He scrubbed a hand through my hair, making me scowl.

'I don't have a hangover.' Leastways, I didn't have the alcohol induced kind. That might have been preferable.

At least I could have cleared that with some orange juice and a dose of Resolve. Emotional migraines weren't quite so easily overcome.

Not the least put off by my hostility, Anthony gave my shoulder a gentle nudge. 'I brought breakfast. Shall we?' He pushed past me to reach the kitchen. 'Just leave the door open. Aaron will only be a minute. He's just grabbing the kit.'

'I forgot you were coming,' I mumbled, following the smell of bacon butties into the kitchen, to find Anthony striding about collecting plates and mugs with which to set the table. Normally the sight of a man in builder's overalls being all domestic would have sparked naughty thoughts, but today it didn't even inspire a smile. I sat down at the breakfast bar, content to let him fuss.

'So, we're thinking we'll get the furniture moved once we've eaten. Then get the old flooring up. After which Aaron and I can dump that and collect the new carpet. We should be done by mid-afternoon – providing there are no distractions.' He gave me a suggestive wink, that I couldn't even be bothered to shake my head at.

My lack of response earned me a look of serious consternation. Anthony poured me a drink. 'Here, get this down you. You look as if you need it.'

The hit of tea did seem to waken my appetite. Leastways, my stomach growled. Somehow, between Nathan's impromptu visit and the fiasco that followed,

I'd failed to eat anything since the lunch I'd shared with Hattie.

Anthony placed a couple of bacon and lettuce filled rolls on a plate and pushed them in front of me, 'Go on, tuck in.'

By the time Aaron swaggered into the room a few minutes later, I was licking smears of ketchup from my fingers and feeling fractionally more sociable, if still rather down.

Whereas Anthony had chosen overalls, Aaron had dressed in ripped jeans and a faded-to-grey band T-shirt that had lost most of its lettering to the washing process. Of course, he still made it look like designer chic. I didn't smile though.

'Morning.' He planted a kiss on my cheek, before sliding onto the next stool. 'So, who won the battle of the titans?'

Anthony groaned, and planted a hand over his face, but his brother paid him no heed.

'What do you mean?' I asked, assuming they were talking about a sporting fixture.

'Well, Nathan paid you a visit last night, didn't he? And you'd arranged to go out with Victor, so I just wanted to know if it came to a punch-up, and if so, who won. That's assuming you didn't just have them both.'

No one had thrown any punches, but I actually felt like thumping him. Normally I didn't mind a bit of ribbing.

It's what came of hanging around with blokes, but last night's events were still too raw to poke at. 'Victor was never here,' I replied tetchily. Not arranging for him to pick me up had probably been my first mistake of the evening.

'But you did go on a date with him?' he asked, not the least bit quelled.

I pushed my stool back. 'I'm going to get dressed. I'm sure you two can find the lounge.'

'Aw, come on, Lys,' Aaron coaxed. He reached out to me as I bumped down off my stool, and caught hold of my hand, which he rubbed soothingly between his palms. 'We just want to know which way you're swinging. It does kind of affect us if you've landed yourself a new man.'

'I haven't.'

He seemed surprised by that admission. 'How come? I'd have thought it'd have been pretty plain sailing.'

Anthony slipped off his stool and walked around the table to take my other hand. While the show of affection soothed some of my irritation, even their combined efforts couldn't alleviate it in its entirety. 'Lyssa, we told Nathan not to come round last night, but you know what a Neanderthal he can be. He can't stand the thought of someone besting him. He doesn't care about what's good for you, only that you're his trophy and Victor's stealing you. I, however, think it's fab if you've found someone else, someone who's into you as a whole person, not just interested because you're so amenable to his whims.'

This was the first time I'd heard either twin speak like this. Though, of course, the times when I'd been completely alone with them were few and far between. Nathan was generally lurking in the vicinity overseeing things.

'I haven't found such a person.' I guess my sadness showed in my face, for Anthony wrapped his arms around me and cradled me against his chest. I thought he was trying to tell me that he'd willingly take that role if I'd only let him, but that he knew deep down my interest didn't match his own.

Meanwhile, Aaron's eyes were narrowed. He thrust his hand into his hair and scratched, causing the blond strands to stick up at unruly angles. 'How come? Victor's obviously besotted with you.'

'Yes, but his boyfriend isn't.'

The reaction to that revelation wasn't what I'd anticipated. I'd expected outraged bleats, particularly as I knew how anti-gay they could all be.

'Did he actually say that to you?' Anthony demanded.

'I overheard them talking.' I didn't elaborate for it dawned on me that neither man seemed surprised to learn that Victor had a lover. 'You knew.' I turned my head from one twin to the other, giving them both hard stares. 'You knew he was already involved. Why didn't you tell me?'

Anthony tugged a pencil from his top pocket and

began thoughtfully sucking on the end. Aaron shifted uncomfortably towards the exit. 'We actually thought you knew. We thought that's why you were so interested. Who wouldn't be motivated by the notion of a threesome with Leif Haralsson?'

There it was – another bomb drop. I just gaped at him. They'd known, not only that Victor was attached, but to whom.

'I guess that wasn't the case,' Aaron mumbled. He grimaced.

'I think you ought to tell me how you knew.'

'Internet. Gossip mags,' they chorused.

I only ever turned the Internet on at home in order to shop, and enough gossip circulated the theatre daily that I never felt the need to fill up on celebrity hearsay.

'The pair of them have been photographed together a zillion times, and there are countless articles about all the threesomes they've supposedly had,' Anthony elaborated.

'Yeah, women seemed to like to document that stuff and then share it with the world.'

That just made Leif's rejection of me worse.

'Did you never think to check him out online?' Aaron asked.

'Do you Google the people you're dating?' I asked incredulously.

'Duh, yeah.' He slapped his forehead. 'If they have sordid secrets, I want to know about them. He doesn't, by the way, at least none besides Leif, who totally isn't a secret.'

I supposed that's why Victor had never mentioned Leif. He probably assumed that I already knew. Not that it mattered now. The episode was over. I just needed to tidy up the remnants of my feelings and bury them in a cupboard.

'Have you spoken to Nathan since last night?' I asked. They were Nathan's mates. He'd probably called them right after he'd left and warned them not to touch me with a ten-foot pole. The only miracle was that they'd still turned up to lay my carpet.

'No. Should we have?'

'It's over between him and me too.'

'Oh!' Aaron's brow furrowed. 'I guess that kind of changes things.' He pulled me to his chest and encompassed me in a hug. Anthony cuddled me too, so that I was surrounded by warmth, my cheek pressed to the thin weave of Aaron's T-shirt that smelled so familiar. For a moment, I genuinely believed that things weren't so bad after all. Still, it was important to ask.

'Are you two leaving me?'

Nathan had warned me that if I finished with him, the others would finish with me.

'It makes things awkward, Lys, I won't deny it.' Aaron's words whispered over the top of my head. I couldn't see the twins, snuggled as I was between their chests, but I suspected some unspoken words were passing between them.

'I think maybe we ought to give you some space.'

As one, they released me, and stepped back.

'So, you are saying goodbye?' I defensively crossed my arms.

'No, it's not that. It's only –' He broke off, shaking his head.

'– we signed a contract,' Anthony finished.

It was my turn to back away. I did so until my back hit the banister in the hallway. I knew we weren't discussing anything to do with carpets or home improvements. No, this was something Nathan had devised. 'He's been selling me,' I said.

Aaron followed me across the tiles. 'There's no fee involved. It's more like a code of conduct. You know how Nathan likes to be in control. Well, that's all it is; a bit of paper that says he gets to be boss and to decide how we do stuff. It's no big deal, Lys.'

It was a big deal. It was a fucking enormous deal.

'Nathan does not make the rules for me.' I was shocked. I was outraged. The reaction hadn't become visceral yet, but I knew it would, and then I was going to be violently sick. 'Do your job,' I yelled. 'Just go and do your job.'

I walked unsteadily to the foot of the stairs. Then, one slow step at a time, I made my way back to bed.

Diary Entry: Thursday 29 July

Dad was right. Men are bastards. And I'm a fool
for not checking the small print.

# Chapter Ten

'You don't have a date tonight? You, don't have a date!' Hattie screeched, so loudly, she turned the heads of the folks browsing the card displays on the opposite side of the theatre foyer. 'But it's Friday. You always go out.'

Hideously embarrassed, I hunched over my work, wishing I could melt into the desk. 'No one to go with,' I muttered, aware that several people were almost certainly eavesdropping.

'Why, where's Nathan?'

I shook my head. The box office wasn't the best place to rake over the still smouldering coals of my relationships, but I could see that Hattie wasn't going to let me maintain any sort of dignity. Her hands were planted firmly on her hips, and deep wrinkles marred her normally smooth brow.

I hadn't bothered to see Nathan in person to challenge him over his 'code'. I'd yelled down the phone. If there'd remained any doubt about our status after Wednesday night, there was none now. We were done, over, never to be rekindled.

'Over, over? Oh, hell,' Hattie muttered when I nodded. 'I think you'd better tell me about it.' She slumped into her office chair, setting it into a slow spin that she stopped with her feet. 'What happened, Lyssa? It was going so well between you.' She grabbed a box of tissues, and then settled her hands into her lap ready to listen. I presumed I was supposed to blubber, but I had no tears in me, none for Nathan anyway. Truthfully, I was more cut up about missing my chance with Victor. Of course, Hattie knew nothing about him and perhaps now wasn't a good time to bring him up.

'Go on,' she coaxed.

Unsure what to say I um'd and ah'd while fiddling with my shirt buttons. 'He did some stuff that wasn't cool ...'

Based on how big and round her eyes went that had been the wrong thing to say.

'Not that bad,' I reassured, giving her hand a gentle pat. I didn't want to give the impression he'd hit me or something. 'Just stuff that wasn't very nice and wasn't what I wanted.'

'Anal?' She nodded sagely, and I had to take one of the damn tissues and pretend to blow my nose just to hide my laughter. I was going to have to consider every word very carefully if I ever went into detail about my former sex life if Hattie considered anal sex a relationship killer. She'd probably spontaneously combust if I told her the whole truth.

Rather than confirming or denying her assumption, I chewed my lip and worked on looking uncomfortable. Maybe if I looked too distraught she'd decide against prodding me for details. There were too many ears still perked up around the foyer.

'Oh, Lyssa, I'm sorry he turned out to be like that.'

So was I. Aaron had emailed me a copy of Nathan's code, which essentially stated that Nathan got to act as he wished, but everyone else had to adhere to the list of prescribed acts or he wouldn't let them play with me. Examples of disallowed acts included multiple men obliging me at the same time, contacting or seeing me without Nathan around unless they had his express permission, and any sort of homosexual contact.

Hattie handed me another tissue that I didn't need, but at least it gave me something to hide behind when an all too familiar figure came jogging down the stairs, and headed straight towards us.

I almost hadn't come into work, but I'd figured Leif would want to avoid me equally as much as I wanted to avoid him. Apparently, I was wrong. I shot out of my seat and wedged myself into the corner by the photocopier before he reached the desk, leaving Hattie to apologise for me.

'She's a bit upset. Split with her boyfriend.'

I could feel Leif's gaze on the back of my neck. He didn't know anything about Nathan, but he knew all too well how things had turned out between me and Victor.

'I'm sorry to hear that.'

Like hell he was. He was probably cheering internally, pleased that Victor had chosen him over me.

'I came down to ask you to a party. The cast are having a get-together next Friday to celebrate the end of the run. I wondered if you two ladies were free to join us? It won't be anything flash, you understand. Just a few drinks at my place.'

That got my attention. Why was Leif inviting me to his house – his house that was also Victor's place?

I turned cautiously, and his laser beam stare caught me straight between the eyes. It was almost hot enough to set my clothes alight. Maybe there wasn't actually a party and he only wanted to get me alone in order to enact some form of hideous revenge. 'You'll come, won't you, Lyssa.' He smiled pleasantly. 'I think you know a friend of mine.'

'No. I don't think so.' I turned swiftly back to my copying and pressed a few random buttons in order to appear busy. The machine spat out copies of the theatre's autumn programme, of which we already had hundreds, but at least sorting them out and stapling them would give me something to do.

'You will come with me, won't you, Lyssa?' Hattie

asked, once Leif was gone. She seemed to have forgotten my woes in favour of jiggling about excitedly. 'I don't really want to go on my own, but I don't want to miss out.'

'I don't know,' I grunted. I couldn't see how anything good would come of it.

'Please. It's the only exciting invite I've had all year.' She linked arms with me. 'And, you know, us singletons really ought to stick together.'

Hattie bugged me all week. She was impossible to say no to, and in the end I had to admit that I was curious. Clearly, Leif had invited me for a reason. The likelihood that he'd had a change of heart and reconsidered Victor's plan was small, but no more far-fetched than any other reason I envisaged. I had to take that chance. I'd have been more confident if I'd heard something from Victor, but he'd never even responded to my goodbye text. I guess with that one word I'd rather slammed the door on us. Retrospectively, maybe I ought to have held off sending it.

'Get a move on, Lyssa.' Hattie called up from the lounge.

I gazed at the sea of outfits that already littered my bed. Nothing was quite right. I had to find the right dress. Something demure enough to make me unremark-able, and yet dressy enough to give the impression I'd made an effort. I wanted to look good enough to eat, but boring enough to blend in.

In the end, I settled for a jade-green dress that fell to mid-thigh level, and wore it with lace-topped stockings and heels. Only if I danced would the lacy detailing show, and I wasn't anticipating dancing. My plan was to find a nice quiet corner and to occupy it, while consuming a nice stiff drink, and to wait and see what happened.

Thumping music greeted Hattie and I as we exited the lift in the exclusive apartment block where Leif and Victor lived. Leif was at the door greeting visitors. He looked ridiculously good; a fact I hated him for. Knowing that he looked equally good, if not better naked, etched a deep grimace onto my face. Hattie gave me a prod, but I couldn't find a smile for her. While she flung herself at Leif, to receive his welcome, I bypassed any form of greeting and sneaked inside.

The place was thrumming. There had to be at least fifty people squeezed into what wasn't a particularly large apartment. That, and I'd learned long ago from working at the theatre, that actors took up additional space. Just two of them could fill a room, not that the guest were all luvvies. There were plenty of backstage and front of house crew too. One or two even called 'hello'.

Having dumped my coat in the prescribed place on the bed in the spare room, I then made straight for the kitchen to grab a drink. One hour, I'd promised Hattie I'd stay, and then I was making my escape. She could follow in her own time.

As the party was post-evening performance, it was already close to midnight, so at least my early departure wouldn't look strange.

I survived twelve minutes in the kitchen, swigging rum and coke, before the presence of the drinks table morphed the room into the central hub of activity. Even that wasn't so bad. Hiding in a crowd was easy. What wasn't so easy was slipping away before being spotted when Victor entered.

Yes, I wanted to speak to him. There were a few things I wanted to say, so he understood I hadn't really stood him up, but any such talk would inevitably lead to further questions, and I didn't want to go airing my dirty laundry in public. Hence, with a great deal of wriggling, and a string of apologies, I managed to circumnavigate the room to the nearest door. Alas it turned out to be the entrance into the utility room and not an alternate route into the lounge.

A bare bulb hung over a basket full of mismatched socks. I turned full circle, but there was no escape. Not even a window to climb through. The door opened and closed behind me, making a quiet snick.

'Lyssa.'

I turned to face Victor, and found all the things that

had originally drawn me to him were still present: his wiry slenderness, the sharp granite-like quality of his jaw, and those pale-as-winter eyes that reminded me of ice on the cusp of melting. He'd dressed in a single-breasted jacket, with a white shirt and tie beneath, and the sight of him took my breath away.

'Do you want to tell me what happened the other night?' he asked, bypassing any sort of social niceties in favour of getting straight to the point.

I chewed my lip, wondering where to start.

Victor crossed to a cupboard and took out a familiar pair of women's shoes. 'These are yours, I believe.'

So he knew.

I gave the tiniest of nods. Having only officially been to his studio once, it was pretty obvious how they'd come to be there, and then there were all those texts I'd sent him saying, 'I'm coming. I'm coming. Nearly there.' It was understandable I'd try his studio once I'd realised he'd left the restaurant.

'How much did you see?'

My tongue traced the sharp edge of my teeth. 'It wasn't what I saw, but what I heard that mattered.'

I hoped he hadn't thought I'd flown because I'd discovered him with another man.

Victor rubbed a hand across his mouth. 'And what was that exactly?'

I took a huge breath. 'That your boyfriend doesn't like

me. That he didn't want you to have anything to do with me. I didn't know about him, by the way. I had no idea you were attached, let alone to him.' I paused having run out of breath. Then, I gave a slow shake of my head. 'I realise it was him you were visiting in the theatre that day too. You didn't even know that I worked there, did you? No wonder you were so jumpy.'

He didn't try to deny it.

'Did you know that Leif had invited me tonight?'

Victor shook his head. I'd rather hoped the invitation had been at his behest.

'And I suppose you've no idea why he'd do that?'

He gave another head shake. 'I love him, Lyssa. I like you … a lot, actually, but you have to understand that I can't sacrifice what I have with Leif for a huge "maybe". I don't even know if you're ever going to be interested in something serious given how many … Well, given how many options you have. I suppose that's why you were late to the restaurant. One of them had different ideas about how you should spend the night.'

'Nathan called,' I said, without elaborating over what had then passed. It wasn't as if Victor and I were set for a reconciliation based on this conversation. I could see it in his eyes, that he'd already let me go.

Time passed. I sat in a corner of Victor's lounge and drank too much. I didn't see Victor again. I saw very little of

Leif, except once, when he seemed to be pairing Hattie up with someone else. I mostly kept clear of my friend. She seemed to be having a great time, and I didn't want to spoil it for her. She looked so happy and beautiful.

Eventually, I think I must have passed out, because I woke feeling dazed to find the lounge in darkness, and only the sound of grunt-like snores in place of music. Actors' bodies littered the room between mounds of party detritus. A quick glance at my phone showed me it was after three. So much for only staying an hour.

I'm pleased to say I was steady on my feet. I didn't know if Hattie was still present and I didn't look for her. She was too sensible to have fallen asleep on a sofa. Besides, I needed to get out of here before daylight came.

Once outside I planned to phone a cab. I almost made it to the front door. That is, I made it to the spare room where I'd left my coat, which was now one of a pitiful few still lying on the miraculously empty bed. It was when I turned that I found Leif standing in the doorway.

Even at three in the morning, he looked just as edible as he had when I'd arrived. On the other hand, I was pretty sure I looked like shit.

'I think we need to chat before you leave.'

Through the thin grey weave of his top, I could make out the tantalising shape of his abdomen. Add to that vision his smoking good looks and eyes that could melt the Snow Queen's heart, and it was no surprise that Victor had chosen him over me. As Victor had rightly put it, I hadn't even offered him exclusivity, and I'd stood him up in favour of someone else on our first proper date.

'Did you see Victor?' Leif asked.

'In the laundry room, a few hours back.'

He frowned at that. Maybe he thought we'd sneaked off to do something wicked.

'I didn't know he had a boyfriend,' I said in my defence. 'It was only when I saw you at the studio I found out.'

I stopped, realising that I'd probably already said too much. I had no idea whether Victor and Leif had actually discussed the details of what had happened. If Leif hadn't been aware of my presence, then he was unlikely to be very happy to learn of it now.

Leif scrubbed a hand through his messy hair. 'Do you know why I invited you tonight? It's because I wanted to meet you properly. You see, I've had several contrasting opinions. Hattie loves you, but you keep big secrets from her. One particular lady at the gallery paints you in a horribly damning light.'

Presumably, said lady was Sam in a tizzy over me dumping Nathan, or maybe jealous of the fact I seemed to have scored with Victor.

'And then there's Victor's opinion.' Leif's tongue flicked against his lower lip. 'His instincts are normally right, and you certainly fire up his libido. I know Victor, Lyssa. I know him very well, and when he gets horny enough to want sex three times a day, that means someone is doing something right.'

I couldn't help smiling. The notion that I'd hot-wired Victor's libido gave me a pleasant glow.

'So I have to conclude that maybe there's a reason for his longing, and maybe I shouldn't have been so hasty to dismiss it. The only thing I don't understand is why you ran the moment the battle-lines were drawn. If you were serious about him, why not stay and fight?'

'I didn't see any possibility of winning. Victor made it plain he'd adhere to your wishes.'

'But only because he thought you'd stood him up. If you'd stepped out of the shadows ... Yes –' he nodded '– I knew you were there, probably from not long after you came in.'

'Then why didn't you say anything?'

'Why didn't you?'

This was all very well, but I didn't see how it changed anything.

'I was cross,' Leif explained. He took a step towards me, and with the bed behind me, I had nowhere to back up to. 'Victor ought to have come to me right away and told me what he wanted. Then we could have talked it through. I'm not saying I'd have agreed, but at least I'd have heard him out and considered it. Instead, after a week of him being all over me, and me thinking I'd inspired those naughty thoughts, it turns out he's actually lusting for someone else, and I'm just a convenient source of relief.'

I had no ready answer to soothe his hurt over the latter half of that sentence, but I could put the first half in perspective. 'We'd known each other less than a week, so it wasn't as if he'd really been keeping things from you. And, we never actually did anything. No sex. No kissing. Mostly we'd talked, and he ...' I was going to say, he watched me do things to myself or with other people, but that would have added several layers of complexity to the matter that didn't need to be discussed.

I thought when Leif began shaking his head that he meant to dismiss me. Instead, he tapped two fingers against his lips. 'Do you want to kiss him?'

I couldn't possibly have heard him correctly. I gave my head a shake just to make sure there was nothing blocking my ears.

'If so, put the coat down.'

And what? What would happen if I dropped my coat back on the bed? Was he seriously suggesting that he was going to escort me to Victor so we could tongue wrestle?

'He's been in a bad place all week, Lyssa, and I don't like seeing him like that. He's been hurt by both of us. So, I've a proposal to sort it out.'

I hardly dared ask what that might be. Luckily, Leif spelled it out anyway.

'We're going to head upstairs and make love to him

together. It'll make a wild end to what's been a somewhat tumultuous night.' Leif held out his hand for me to grasp.

It seemed I'd fallen into some parallel universe, or else I was dreaming this. Cautiously, I put my coat back on the bed, and then accepted Leif's hand. It felt real enough. His palm was warm and huge. It enveloped mine completely. The possibility of finally being able to hold Victor beat a thundering path across my synapses. 'Wait.' I halted Leif by the foot of the stairs. Even with the possibility of finally being able to hold Victor firing like a twenty-one gun salute, I was still compos mentis enough to realise, 'You weren't … You didn't want to do this.'

Leif bowed his head, which still didn't bring him down to my height. 'I'm not saying this is going to be a permanent arrangement, Lyssa. Let's just see what happens tonight.' He gently ruffled my hair. 'How about a kiss to cement the deal and prove I'm willing?' He didn't actually wait for an answer. There was no hesitation in him. In many ways, Leif was the complete antithesis of Victor. I guess that's why they matched up so well.

His mouth descended onto mine. His tongue gently stroked my lips, teasing, toying before seeking entry. Panic trickled through me when I thought of Hattie. She was going to kill me for this, assuming I didn't expire from joy first, because, boy did this man know how to kiss. But that fear alone wasn't enough to make me give up this opportunity. If I wanted Victor, then Leif came as part of the deal. I was just going to have to do a hell of a lot of grovelling.

We played, tongues sparring for several long minutes until lack of oxygen forced us apart. By then we were both panting.

My gaze dropped to Leif's loins. I could have kicked myself when I heard him chuckle. 'Still doubting I'm really up for it. Run your hand across my fly and I guarantee you'll find me hard.' He squeezed my bum, cupping the cheeks in his big hands, so I did the same to him.

'Mm, are you up for it too?'

I was. I definitely was.

Leif gave his hips a suggestive wiggle as I dug my fingers a little deeper into the firm muscles of his flanks. 'Now, let's find Victor.'

The master bedroom sat on a mezzanine floor above the lounge. The only furniture was the bed and a basket-like chair that hung from the ceiling. Several items of male clothing littered the floor; things that I recognised as Victor's. They seemed to lead to an adjoining door, through which the patter of water could be heard.

'Seems like he's cleaning up.' Leif crossed to the door and tried the handle. For a moment, I thought he intended us to crowd into the bathroom and join Victor under the spray. Instead, he asked, 'Are you going to be long?'

'A minute or three.'

Leif closed the door. 'You heard him. We have a minute

or three.' Until, Victor presumably waded out of there wearing nothing but a towel and asked what the hell I was doing in his bedroom. Now that I was here, I was having doubts about this plan. Things had been decidedly awkward between Victor and I earlier. Reacquainting ourselves on a more convivial level might be sensible before trying to dive headlong into a threesome.

'Don't fret, sweetheart.' Leif enfolded me in a bear hug. Maybe he was drunk, though he didn't taste of alcohol. 'It's going to be fine. Let's work on getting to know one another.'

I'd only known Leif a few minutes, but I'd already decided he was a dangerous man. He had a way of persuading you into things that oughtn't to have worked, but somehow did when he said them in his silky smooth drawl.

He nibbled my earlobe, and then traced his tongue down the side of my neck, raising shivers of excitement. 'This way he'll believe me when I tell him I've changed my mind, because it'll be obvious how into you I really am.'

Nothing proved consent like hot action.

Leif pulled me tight to his chest. My back pressed to his loins, so that his erection nuzzled against my cheeks. I hadn't taken him up on his offer downstairs, but I felt his arousal now. Maybe in the end this wasn't even about Victor and me, just about Leif wanting to get laid. Perhaps I was the only woman left in the building. Not that I was implying Leif didn't make me feel special. Actually, the moment his lips sealed over my pulse point a separate heartbeat took up lodgings in my sex. I whimpered, and ground back against him. A week and a half without sex and I was as mad for him.

I was facing the bathroom door when Victor emerged. His dark hair was brushed back against his scalp, and the wet ends were dripping into the collar of the robe he'd fastened over the towel around his waist.

'Leif? Lyssa? W-what's going on?' He folded his arms.

'I want to get laid tonight. I brought a girl back. I hope you don't mind.' Leif ran his hands over the front of my dress. He explored the curve of my belly and then the swell of my breasts. 'Don't you think she's beautiful, Victor? Will you share her with me?'

In response Victor tightened his robe more firmly. Stop it, I wanted to say. Can't you see that he's annoyed? But at the same time I craved him so much that I prayed there was a sliver ... just a sliver of chance ... that'd he'd fall in with Leif's plan.

'How come you're suddenly OK with this?' he asked Leif. 'You do know who she is?'

'Of course I do. I invited her.'

'Then why?'

'Simple.' Leif rested his chin against my shoulder in order to look across at his lover. 'I reconsidered, thought things over a bit, and decided that maybe I was being unreasonable. It's not as if there's any harm in testing things out.' He straightened to his full height, and moved aside my hair so that he could unzip my dress. 'You have a point. It would be nice to have someone we both liked and trusted around to satisfy that certain itch we both share in bed. The after-party gossiping does get irritating. I don't want to read about how my dick is two inches shorter than yours and how when I come I sound like a steam kettle.'

'You don't sound like a steam kettle.'

'Somebody thought I did.'

'I'm still not …' Victor stared as Leif removed my dress and bra, and began snapping open the clips of my garter belt. 'Fuck!' he murmured, when Leif's hand covered my pussy and his middle finger pressed between the folds of my sex. I was dripping wet; eager and yet still half believing. If it hadn't been for Leif's strong arms around me, I'd probably have melted right into the carpet.

'Dammit, Leif! Stop. This is mental. I've never even touched her and you're … you're all over her.' Victor's eyes were eating me up as he followed the subtle and not so subtle movements of Leif's fingers. Victor surreptitiously adjusted his robe.

'So stop gaping and come and get your fingers wet.'

Leif pushed down my panties. Then he smoothed his palms over the long muscles of my thighs, first down the outsides, then up the inners until his fingers opened me to Victor.

Victor didn't move. He seemed rooted to the spot.

'I'm going to have her.' The rumble of Leif's promise vibrated through my back and sent a shiver of excitement racing across my body. 'I'm going to slide into her and ...' His abs tightened as his hips swayed against me. Between that pressure against my back and the continued stroking of his fingers inside my sex, I was rapidly becoming desperate for him to do exactly that.

'It's what you ought to have done instead of making that half-arsed attempt at being loyal and faithful.' Leif chose that moment to not only land a finger on my clit, but to suckle on the love bite he'd already left on my neck. A desperate, affirmative groan rolled up my throat.

I swear the guy had magic fingertips, because despite how uncomfortable Victor looked, I wanted Leif to carry on.

I wanted Victor too. I wanted him to come and tear Leif off me and make his own mark upon my neck.

'Leif.' The anxiety in Victor's voice made it sound as though it came up from his toes. He tightened and flexed his fists, but didn't make any move towards me.

'What?' his lover asked. 'No one is stopping you. All you need do is take a step ... two steps. Rub up against her front. Kiss her. Let her feel the snake you're hiding under that towel. Meanwhile, I'm going to find me some fun down here.' Leif's kisses pitter-pattered down my spine as he knelt. He began to nuzzle against my butt, squeezing the globes tight together then releasing them. The tip of his tongue flicked across one cheek. The next thing I knew, he was licking into the channel and seeking out the tight furl of muscle hidden there.

I couldn't keep still with him doing that. With nothing else to cling to, I reached out to Victor for support. He still stood too far away.

'What's he doing to you?' he asked.

The basics of it had to be apparent, given our relative positions and how impossible I was finding it not to squirm. I felt Leif's grin against my cheeks as his tongue continued to dance around that sensitive furl of muscle.

'He's doing that ...'

Leif extended his fingers, and pushed two into the heat of my sex. As he slipped them in and out, his tongue made a similar foray into my behind.

'And he's doing that ... Oh, yes,' I whimpered.

'You like that?' Leif asked. 'Then maybe we'll come back to that.' He stopped licking and concentrated instead on sliding a third finger in alongside the two that were already ploughing my pussy. 'Oh, Victor. She's so ripe, and so willing. Talk to him, Lyssa. Tell him what you want.'

'Please,' I moaned. I didn't know what else to say. I'd wanted Victor right from the first glimpse of him I'd seen in that gaudy mirror at the gallery. I thought it had all ended between us, but now Leif was offering a lifeline, and we'd be fools not to accept it. 'Just, please.

Come and hold me. Touch me. Don't hold back. Just let it happen.'

'That's right, Victor. Just let it happen. Don't over-think it.' Leif's hair tickled as he pressed a kiss to my thigh. 'Tell him what to do. Make him take that ridiculous robe off.'

'Will you take it off?' I asked.

For one harrowing moment, I thought he would refuse. His shoulders bunched up and torment seemed to infuse his pale eyes. 'Please, Victor.' His teeth raked over his lower lip, but he undid his belt. Then, teasingly he turned his back on us before shrugging off the robe and releasing the towel.

'If you haven't learned it yet, he's a right bloody tease,' Leif whispered conspiratorially.

Victor responded by casting a sultry glance over his shoulder that seemed to say 'If you want more. You'd better be nice'.

I didn't mind Victor teasing, so long as he was on board with this. 'Turn around,' I pleaded.

'Yes, much as I love your arse, Vic, be a sport and turn around. Let the lady see what you've got for her.'

Victor turned but with his arm strategically placed over his loins.

Thoroughly tormented, I hissed through my teeth.

He uncovered. Then rolled his hips as if to ask, 'You like?'

I did indeed like. He was as I remembered, thin and

wiry; his cock slender like the rest of him, but several shades darker in tone. But regardless of how lush I found Victor's body, admiring him wasn't my primary motive for getting him naked. The thing with being naked is that you can't hide. Everything is out in the open, and I wanted the three of us to be completely honest about this.

Meanwhile, Leif began stroking into me faster. I think he was toying with the idea of adding a fourth finger into the mix. The thumb of his other hand was already working my nub, causing the tight little bead to give off lightning darts of pleasure.

'Come,' I begged Victor, beckoning him closer. If it wasn't for Leif's activity, I'd have stumbled forward and smothered Victor in countless kisses, or else just fallen at his feet and worshiped his very long and very lovely erection.

This time he took a step forward. 'Touch me. Kiss me,' I begged.

'He should take your nipples in his mouth and suck you,' Leif suggested. 'I bet you'd like that.'

'I'd rather see him come over them.'

My honesty sparked coughs from both men.

'You're really rather dirty,' Leif remarked. 'I love it.' He nodded at Victor. 'Now I'm beginning to understand.' He stood and set about nibbling the side of my neck again. I gathered it was a favourite point of his, yet his attention didn't stay there for long. A moment later, his hand once again cupped my pussy, and his middle finger began stroking between the lips of my slit. He caught the underside of my clit every time he jerked his hips forward. Each thrust also buried his cock a little deeper between the seam of my buttocks. I was silky wet back there, slicked by his juices, so that the eager jerks met with little resistance. With only minor adjustments he could probably slide right into me.

I think Victor realised that too, for his tongue flicked out and passed quickly across his teeth. Liquid fire seemed to burn across the icy surface of his eyes. He reached up to me as if he meant to cup my cheek, though he stopped short of actual contact. Instead, I had to strain towards the caress. Despite everything Leif was doing, I was Victor's first, if he'd only claim me.

'I'm totally primed,' Leif muttered to himself. He stopped humping my rear, and started fishing about in his pockets. A moment later he had a condom in his hand and was making swift work of the packaging. His erection was kissing his abs as he rolled the sheath into place. Unlike Victor and I, Leif still had all his clothes on. 'Time to get your butt on the bed.' He slapped my bottom playfully. 'Lady, have I got something fab lined up for you.'

Now Victor, I begged looking right into his eyes. Why are you still holding back?

Maybe after all, he was predominantly a voyeur.

'You two might consider kissing before we do the dirty,' Leif prompted. He began stripping off his remaining clothing, which included stepping out of the black jeans that were clinging to his thighs. The floor beneath us had turned into a multi-coloured jumble of discarded clothes.

Victor's fingers finally made contact with my cheek. His thumb brushed down over my parted lips making them tingle.

'I want to taste you.'

'Likewise.'

'And touch you.' I reached out to trace the outline of his cock, but he caught hold of my hand.

For a second or two, he explored the contours of my palm, then he guided me towards my goal. 'Gently. Super gently. Too much and I will lose it.' He closed his eyes as I stroked him. 'Oh, Lyssa. You don't know how much I've longed for this.'

Only I did, because I'd craved him too.

I felt his groan in my gut. Then, finally, finally, his lips brushed mine in a whisper-soft caress. My senses screamed.

'Mmm.' He feasted more deeply. His kiss bore certain nuances that reminded me of Leif. Only Victor was more fervent and his hunger more apparent. All the desperation and longing of the last two weeks fed into the dance of our tongues and the flexing of my fist around his cock.

Abruptly, Victor's stomach muscles crunched. Then

equally hurriedly, he fought off my grip. Alarm danced in his eyes, as he stood before me panting hard.

'Easy there. Breathe.' Leif gave Victor's balls a gentle downwards tug, before tightening his fingers around the base of his lover's erection. 'I know it's exciting. But there's no need to go off just yet. Just relax a little. Go easy on him, Lyssa.'

# *Chapter Eleven*

'This way, honey.' Leif led me by the hand over to the low futon-style bed. Victor held my other hand, our fingers locked tight. Finally, I was starting to believe this might all work out. I didn't want to let go of Victor, not even to climb onto the bed.

Leif lay on his back and had me straddle him. 'You've done this before, right?'

No – no, I hadn't. I'd wanted to, and enjoyed plenty of fantasies about it happening. I was even used to the dance of multiple limbs and how it was possible to arrange one body next to another without most of them touching. But, I'd never actually welcomed two men together. Hence, while I could kid myself I knew what I was doing, I had no practical experience.

I shook my head, only to realise he'd been joking regarding his expectation of experience.

'How do you feel about us both being in you? Is that something you're up for?'

'I'm up for whatever you've got.'

'We don't have to rush into this,' Victor said. 'There are other ways.'

I already knew what it felt like to be rubbed against. To have one man massaging me, or kissing me while another filled me up. What I craved, was the step beyond that. The thing Leif was offering. I'd never before been with two men comfortable enough with one another to even attempt it. Now that I had found two such men, I wasn't going to let the moment slip by out of fright.

'I trust you,' I whispered to Victor. I was sure he'd keep me safe.

Leif squeezed my thigh. 'Turn around and face Victor.'

Victor kissed me. He kissed me until I was jittery and overeager. Then kissed me until I relaxed, and while he did so, he explored every inch of my body. He covered me, bore me down against Leif, whose hands caressed and tormented me too. Their mingled breaths whispered against my neck, one either side. When they sought each other's mouths over my shoulder, it stirred something visceral inside me, and further raised my pulse.

Victor's erection rubbed against my stomach. Leif's insistently against my rear. I was ready for more, but when I tried to grab them, tried to guide them, they clasped my hands over my head and prevented me from directing anything.

'Ah-ah. Not yet,' directed Leif.

'But I need you? I want ...'

Victor stroked down between my pussy lips and unsurprisingly found me sopping. 'So, you do. So, you do.' He licked his fingers. I think I almost jackknifed upwards. I thought he would enter me then. He was ridiculously hard, more than ready, but it wasn't his cock that jutted up between my legs to rub my sex from behind. Victor guided his lover into place, until I was clutching at Leif's erection, drawing him into me.

Victor sat back and watched. He stroked my breasts, squeezed and sucked the nipples into points. Then he touched himself. He made a fist around his shaft and rubbed much harder than I thought he could possibly tolerate. Each time his hand closed over the head, the following downward swish sounded a little stickier.

Between the sight of him, and the feel of Leif, prod, prod, prodding away at my entrance, but never sliding more than an inch or two inside, my nerves were shredded. 'Aah – more!' I wanted it harder. This was torture, sweet, heavenly torture, but torture nonetheless. I clawed at Victor's thighs, tried to pull him to me. I tilted my hips, desperate to get Leif inside me a little deeper. Oh God, it felt so good!

A hum had started inside my pussy. Leif wasn't in me very deeply, but the angle pushed him up against a maddeningly sensitive spot that sent tingles out that amplified the buzz in my clit. Very soon, that alone was going to make me come. 'Victor,' I begged. I fought against Leif's continued hold on my wrists. I knew we were going to have to switch around if they were both going to fill me.

'Easy, Lyssa. There's no rush.' Victor knelt astride me. His hot hands ran up my thighs, stroking and squeezing. I did the same to him, enjoying the tickle of soft hairs against my palms. 'Let me taste you a little first. I've wanted to, you know, ever since you first showed me what you had down here.' His head drew level with my hips. Then his tongue peeped out and tickled my pearl.

My cunt clenched tight around Leif's shaft. No way, would any of my former lovers have performed such an act. It would have put them too close to another man's bits. Victor, I swear, did it because it allowed him to taste us both. Each time he spared a lick for Leif, I felt the resulting jolt.

Leif finally let go of my wrists. I think he was finding Victor's attention a little too sweet as well. His breath was rough against my ear. His fingers found my nipples, pinched and twisted as he continued to fill me. And he was filling me now, driving up into me, going deep.

That just seemed to spur Victor to suck a little harder. My tiny nubbin was so hard now. I thought I would never come, that I would hit a wall and be unable to pass through.

How wrong I was. Victor slipped a finger inside of me, right alongside Leif and it toppled me completely.

By the time the feathery pulses had stopped I was boneless and mewling like a day old kitten. The climax had left me sopping.

'I think we're ready now.' Victor sat back on his haunches. I don't think I really understood what he meant, until he was over me.

How was this …? It couldn't work. We were all twisted around the wrong way. Leif was still inside me, so Victor was going to have to go in my rear, but that was sandwiched against Leif's loins.

Only it did happen. Just not the way I expected it. Victor pressed his erection downwards so that his cock rested parallel to Leif's. Without rushing he edged forwards. Then on the next thrust he was prodding at my entrance, and with the next he was inside of me, sandwiched inside my pussy right beside Leif, and the pair of them were filling me in a way I'd never even imagined.

My sense of reality vanished. All that mattered was the rub and thrust. I was hot all over; Leif and Victor two infernos heating me both inside and out. Everything was too snug, borderline claustrophobic. I couldn't quite catch my breath.

Yet, I didn't want it to end, as attested to by the constant roll of my hips.

This time my orgasm crept up so fast it seemed to

arrive completely without warning. Nerves fired, my muscles twitched and set off a chain reaction of similar spasms right across my body.

Apparently all that squeezing was too much for the men. 'Oh, hell,' Victor swore. 'I can't hold it.' His next few thrusts were all over the place, his seed lubricating the way. No sooner was he spent than Leif was coming too, shouting and cursing through gritted teeth.

Finally spent, we collapsed into a smiley, lethargic heap.

The reality of what we'd done didn't sink in until hours later, when I woke bleary eyed to find the sun long risen and my body sore. Leif was nowhere to be seen, but Victor still lay snuggled beside me. I pressed my head to his chest and listened to the sound of his heartbeat.

He stirred within a minute or two. 'Lyssa?' His arm tightened around my shoulders giving me a squeeze. After a moment, he sought my lips too. 'How are you? Are you OK? We weren't too rough with you.'

'I'm fine,' I said, but I wasn't. I was too content in his arms, too willing to lie there and never leave, but I still didn't know if that was an option. Hence, I was frightened, desperately frightened.

'Hey.' Victor sat us up when he felt my tears against his skin. 'Don't cry. What's the matter?' He rubbed my show of sadness away.

'What will he say?' I asked. Leif's absence had to be a

bad sign. 'Where's he gone?' He wasn't in the adjoining bathroom, we'd have heard him.

'He's probably surveying the wreckage downstairs. No doubt it looks even worse now than it did last night.'

Victor's suggestion was reasonable, but I had no cause to expect another miracle to occur so soon. In many ways the events of the previous night remained inexplicable enough.

'He's house-proud, you know. He likes it to look like a show home.' Victor relaxed against the pillows and pulled me to him.

'Is that why your studio is such a muddle, because you're protesting against the order?'

He pursed his lips. 'Maybe something like that, or it could just be that I don't tidy up.'

'You don't seem worried,' I observed.

'I'm not. Whatever he says, I'm not going to give you up. Someway we'll come up with a compromise.'

It was another half an hour before Leif finally came up the stairs. I sat up straight, my hand clasped tight around Victor's.

'Morning slugabeds.' Leif breezed into the room. He was wearing cut-off denim shorts and a garish blue, green and gold dragon print T-shirt. 'The house is a wreck and the gannets have been in the kitchen, but I managed to save you some food.' He gave a theatrical bow and placed the tray loaded with bagels, cream cheese and orange juice across our laps. 'Will there be anything else?'

'Coffee,' Victor croaked.

'We're out.'

'Aren't you going to tuck in?' Leif asked a moment later, when neither Victor nor I had moved. He snatched one of the bagels and took a huge bite. 'What?'

We both continued to stare at him.

'Lyssa would like to know where she stands. Is she welcome, Leif?'

His brow wrinkled, for a moment he appeared baffled. Then he broke into an enormous smile. 'You two.' He punched us both in the shoulders. 'Do you think I'd have made you breakfast if you weren't? Of course she's welcome. In fact, after I've showered, I think I might be up for a repeat.'

184